THE GODMOTHER

The Sicilian Housewife Diaries
2012

Veronica Di Grigoli

Foreword

Some years ago I visited Sicily for a wedding, and accidentally fell in love with one of the groom's three hundred or so cousins. I plucked up the courage to leave my family and friends in London, give up my career, sell my house, car and collection of seventies disco albums and move to a fishing village in northern Sicily with a population of about six hundred people (several of whom do still have their own teeth). Everyone, Sicilians included, kept asking me how I could do what I did. It was not a simple question to answer, so I started writing my Dangerously Truthful Diary of a Sicilian Housewife as a blog, to try to explain.

I have told the story of meeting my husband, getting married and having our son in the travel novel "The Dangerously Truthful Diary of a Sicilian Housewife". That book ended when my son was born, and this new book contains all my diary entries from 2012 when my son was six years old. This was the year Sicily's immigration crisis from Africa was just beginning, the Olympics were held in London, the Queen had her Diamond Jubilee and you couldn't buy a mug, apron or jar of chutney without a Union Jack on, Barack Obama was the president of America, Mario Monti was the president of Italy and Silvio Berlusconi was reminiscing at home about his lascivious bunga bunga parties.

In 2012 almost every object for sale in England told you to Keep Calm and do something or other. Meanwhile I was living in Sicily, and nobody was keeping calm about anything.

ISBN: 9781799186465

Ten Sicilian Clichés: True or False?

My hubby thinks I should perpetuate all the classic clichés about Sicily in my blog. He reckons this will guarantee a loyal readership.

"Tell them your husband is four feet tall. Tell them he wears a flat cap and a white vest, with splatters of tomato sauce on it, and chest hairs spilling out of the top."

"OK," I agreed.

We were discussing my blog over dinner. He was full of ideas that I should include in my "blob", as he called it. (His English is still not too great. I have only been working on it for eight years. I have calculated that, if I keep this up at a steady rate, he will be fluent by his 103rd birthday).

He made me promise to claim that he rules the household with a rod of iron and never lifts a finger. I am to report that he does not know how to make his own coffee. I must also claim that we travel around by donkey.

This set me thinking about the nature of stereotypes. Why do we love them so much? Perhaps they make us feel we always know what we are dealing with. After all, the unknown and the unpredictable can be very intimidating. Or perhaps we use our stereotypes about others to define *ourselves*: We construct our own identity by contrasting ourselves with all the people we are NOT.

We decided to investigate further by composing a list of the top ten Sicilian clichés.

1. Sicilians are all midgets.

This actually used to be true. The oldest generation does indeed consist of men who look like garden gnomes come to life, and women whose pelvic bone is wider than they are tall, so that they can rock down the road looking like a catamaran. Nowadays this generation is dying out. It takes a sharp eye to spot them. The average young Sicilian is taller than the average mainland Italian. Lots of them are gigantic. Long gone are the days when Sicilian kitchens were fitted with a sink that normal people could use as a bidet.

Why were they so small back then? They were children during the Second World War. Many Sicilians died of starvation, and those who survived suffered severe childhood malnutrition, which seriously stunted their growth. I met a lady in hospital who told me about the bread they could get during the war. She said it seemed to have sawdust and sand to bulk it out and was so full of holes you could see through it. She described to me calmly, and matter-of-factly, the effects of malnutrition on the children of her generation and listed one by one the names of her classmates who had died of starvation. She had tears in her eyes at this point and told me,

"I always say their names to make sure they know they are not forgotten." She said she recovered fairly well but her younger brother suffered from intestinal damage his whole life, was seriously stunted and never recovered his health.

2. Sicilians are all in the Mafia.

There are 5 million people living in Sicily. An estimated 1,700 of them - one in three thousand - is in the Mafia, apparently. That means 99.967 % of Sicilians are NOT in the Mafia. But be careful when you meet one! Because you never know...

3. Sicilian women all wear black.

It's a total myth that old Sicilian women wear black all the time. They only wear it when they want to look sexy. They mostly wear velour tracksuits (always a size too small) in shocking pink, or very tight T-shirts encrusted with sequins and diamanté and hipster jeans with significant muffin-top overspill. In the old days, when a woman was widowed, she went into mourning and stayed in it for the rest of her life. And, thanks to the Second World War, there used to be lots of widows in Sicily.

Nowadays they love to wear black for smart occasions, most notably weddings. Even if the wedding is in the morning, the women all dress in black evening dresses - with diamanté and sequins on. But nobody uses it for everyday wear.

4. Sicilian boys cannot kiss or touch the girls before they are married.

I do actually know a few parents who wish this were the case. I don't know any teenagers who care.

5. Sicilian men wear white vests.

Well, my husband does. I once teased him about this and he rather huffily defended it, calling it *la camicia della salute* – the "shirt of health". It keeps him warm under his shirt from the bitter winds of winter, and offers ideal, cool ventilation in the roasting heat of summer. But he only wears it inside the house. The only time you will see a white vest out in public is when it's hanging on the washing line.

My actual husband

6. Sicilian women have moustaches.

The Sicilians brought this stereotype upon themselves with their old saying, "Donna baffuta sempre piaciuta", which translates as "A woman with a moustache has always been pleasing". Despite my constant vigilance, I have yet to spot a single woman with errant facial hair here in Sicily. Perhaps they do have hair growth, but the two litres of concentrated perfume they use to douse their faces every morning dissolves the follicles away?

Donna baffuta

7. Sicilian men are the world's worst male chauvinists.

My husband constantly brings home delicious foods cooked by his male colleagues. (He pretends to work hard but they actually sit about in the office exchanging recipes.) My neighbours seek permission from their wives before leaving the house for whatever purpose, be it going for a jog or even popping out to buy a loaf of bread. *Mamma mia!* Most Sicilian men hand over their whole pay check to their wife, as the woman of the house is in charge of spending the money. This is the land of Mummy's boys. Women reign supreme in this culture. Mamma knows best. Always.

The thing I find most touching of all about Sicilian men is their utter devotion as fathers. It is very commonplace to see a man out for a walk, pushing a baby along in a pram. He will proudly stop to show off his latest child or grandchild to all admirers, wrapped in an exuberant array of pink embroidered covers adorned with lacy frills. Most of them are skilled at changing nappies, good at mixing bottles of formula and burping the baby afterwards, and love teaching the *bambino* new words.

In Sicilian churches, you are just as likely to see a statue of Joseph holding baby Jesus, as you are to see depictions of Mary and Jesus. Whilst Sicilians adhere to the cult of the Virgin Mary as enthusiastically as any other Catholics, they attach equal importance to the love and dedication of Joseph, the father who married Mary knowing she was already pregnant, and proudly raised baby Jesus as his own son.

Buon appetito!

8. Sicilians eat spaghetti with tomato sauce every single day.

This is completely untrue. There are many other shapes of pasta that they eat to vary their diet. Some days they have fusilli, sometimes farfalle, or conchiglie... the variety is endless.

9. Sicilian women are not allowed out of the house without a chaperone.

Not at all true. However, in some traditional families, the girls would not be allowed to go and live in their own apartment before getting married. They would not be allowed to sleep outside the family home unless under the roof of a trusted adult... since that would mean their reputation had been soiled. This gave rise to the great Sicilian tradition of the *fuitina*.

Basically, two love-struck teenagers whose parents are refusing to let them marry, will run away from home for a few days. When they return, it is assumed that the girl has been deflowered, so the parents will force the young man to marry her in order to restore her reputation – which was of course the objective of the whole venture in the first place. This does still happen very occasionally. It is a case of some teenagers being able to take advantage of parents with particularly archaic morals. It will certainly die out with the next generation, as there is nobody in the younger generation who would feel losing your virginity means you ought to get married.

10. Sicilians are very dark skinned, in fact they are really North Africans.

This is a stereotype that many north Italians love to perpetuate. They love to call Sicilians "Africans", implying they are a different race from "real" Italians and therefore don't deserve any regional investment of nationally gathered tax revenues.

In reality, Sicily has been occupied so many times, by so many different races and empires, that there is no typical Sicilian look. You get blondes, brunettes, black haired people, brown eyes, green eyes... there are examples of everything here. Even some good-looking people if you hunt hard enough...

8

So there you have it. The low-down on the real Sicily of today.

If I am right that we use clichés to define what we are NOT, or at least what we do not want to be, then that means we like to see ourselves as tall and svelte, well-dressed, modern-thinking and persistent eaters of varied and healthy food. Well, fine! That works for me!

Anyway I had better go now, because my husband wants me to make him some spaghetti with tomato sauce. I need to iron his vest, comb my moustache and veil my face before I serve him. On my knees, as he is so short.

The Godmother

My Sicilian mother-in-law is nicknamed The Godmother in some circles.

She is a major hub of the Auntienet. Old women in Sicily don't need Internet connections like Twitter or Facebook or any of that nonsense. They have had the Auntienet for generations. The Auntienet is a network of elderly female relatives and godmothers, which can convey interesting or scandalous information in "real time". Sicilian children dare not swear in public or pat dirty stray dogs, as The Godmothers Are Watching and their parents will already have devised a punishment before they can get home. The Auntienet is a social network with spanking power.

Anyway, without further ado, let me present my mother-in-law and some of the other main routers and switches of the Auntienet.

THE GODMOTHER

> Likes: Making children eat more than their body weight in food before she lets them leave the table
>
> Dislikes: Priests who make mass last less than three hours
>
> Special skill: Stuffing a chicken inside a turkey inside a lamb and roasting it on a spit

My mother-in-law is a fairly typical Sicilian woman of the older generation. When her mansize hands are not busy flaying and massacring vegetables or scrubbing household objects to the brink of oblivion, they fiddle with rosary beads. She goes to church twice on Sundays and is godmother to seven children. **The Godmother**. You would not want to be naughty in her presence. Her hands could probably spank even a decent-sized adult man into geostationary orbit, if he deserved it.

In case you are worried, I think I am safe to speak openly because my husband only speaks broken English mixed with German, French and Expletive, and the only English word that The Godmother knows is "cuppatino", which is a cappuccino made using a teabag instead of coffee.

SIGNORA ANNA

> Likes: Scrubbing children's faces clean with a technique American plastic surgeons think they invented, and call "dermabrasion"
>
> Dislikes: People who say "hello" to her when she is studying them from behind her net curtains
>
> Special skill: Hanging her laundry up from a washing line strung between her window shutters and a nearby lamppost

Signora Anna lives in the flat downstairs from the Godmother's, and they have some special means of communication so rapid it probably relies on telepathy.

Likes: Indoctrinating children in the ways of the Lord

Dislikes: People who say they are on a diet

Special skill: Hoisting loaves of bread up three storeys using a basket tied to twenty metres of rope dangling from her kitchen balcony

Well, there you have it, a sampling of the good Godmothers of Sicily! God bless them, and long may they live to make sure the kids are brought up and fed properly!

A Chat in Sicilian

One is not particularly amused

Many Sicilians, when you ask them if they speak Sicilian, look at you as if they are the Queen on a royal walkabout and you just said,

"Go on, Your Majesty, pull my finger."

Quite why they find it so insulting is something I have still not fully fathomed. All I can tell you is that they are always the ones who think they are posh. They would definitely claim to be "*Upper* middle class," if such an English way of thinking could be expressed in their language.

The thing that makes this most mysterious of all is that, later, you notice that more than half their status updates on Facebook are written in pure Sicilian.

Meanwhile the working class people speak Sicilian all the time, and get fairly muddled if you ask them to speak Italian. The older they are, the worse it is. Some of them manage one sentence in Italian then revert to Sicilian; others just give up speaking altogether and fall into that enigmatic, observant silence that elderly Sicilians pull off with such dignity.

I had a whole conversation with an old man this morning in Sicilian. We chatted for about five minutes. I've no idea what he said. Absolutely none.

Sicilian is a fun language though. I like speaking it, not only for the guffaws it always produces when people hear my English accent, but also because.... Well, see for yourself.

Here's a bit of Sicilian:

Camurria means a terrible drag, or an interminable nuisance. For example, getting stuck in a traffic jam is a camurria; having to take a day off work and wait at home for the man from British Gas to come "sometime between 9am and 6pm" is a camurria; an even bigger camurria is having to wait for the

Sicilian gas man to come "some time between Monday morning and Thursday afternoon, probably."

Fitusu (pronounced fitoozoo) means stinky, gone off and disgusting.

Piciotti (pronounced pichotti) is a great word simply because most Italians think it means a Mafia member of the most junior level. What it really means in Sicilian is Lads, or young men. So groups of young men will call each other piciotti, as in "Come on Piciotti, let's go and get some ice-cream and try to pick up some chicks".

Piciriddu (pronounced pitchiriddoo) is the little version of piciotti. It means child.

Sicilian is a very earthy language. It is equipped with multiple words for different types of farts. The sort that comes out loud and proud is called a **Piritu**. (Someone who puts on airs and graces may be called "an *inflated piritu*".) The type you manage to sneak out secretly, if necessary by breaking it down into several smaller sections, is a **sgurreggiu**. The type which mean you have to rush off urgently and change your underwear is called a **Luffione**. I won't list any more, just in case the Queen is reading...

Sicilian pasta with lentils... very prone to producing Piriti, and occasionally luffioni

Children from full-time Sicilian speaking families do have a reasonable grounding in Italian before they start primary school, but they struggle when they enter an academic environment and have to use Italian exclusively, for writing, for speaking, and for studying. They are learning a lot of new vocabulary, as well as the subject being taught. They must find it a real *camurria*. Throughout their school careers they are told off if they utter a word of Sicilian in class.

Many a time I have been chatting to other teachers, who have gone off on a bit of a moan about the amount of Sicilian the kids talk in class.

"You do tell them off whenever they speak Sicilian, don't you?" they say.

"I tell them off when they speak Italian," is my usual answer, "since I teach English."

I feel uneasy telling Sicilians not to use their mother tongue.

My father grew up in a Wales which was in danger of losing its language. Both his grandmothers had badly scarred hands from being beaten every time they spoke Welsh at school – even when they were too young to have learnt any English. One of them remained so deeply traumatised that, once she had managed to grasp English, she was too afraid to speak Welsh ever again, even inside her own home as a married woman. This was the result of a deliberate policy by the English to eradicate the Welsh language. The children of Wales were taught that their language was inferior and their only hope of ever getting on in life was to stop speaking it, and learn English instead.

Having made the language so obscure it was on the brink of dying out, the British government had no hesitation in using it for military purposes in wartime. The signallers of the Royal Welch Fusiliers sent messages in Welsh during the Second World War and in the war in Bosnia, for example. Welsh looks so unpronounceable written down that apparently the Germans spent months trying to crack the code, thinking they were intercepting messages in an encrypted form of English.

The Welsh adopted measures to save their language in the nick of time. It is now one of the flourishing minority languages in Europe. In 1993, a law in Wales decreed that English and Welsh must be treated equally in all public sector institutions. This means that hospitals must be able to provide Welsh speaking doctors and nurses, for example, and all government websites are available in Welsh and English. The ability to speak Welsh is compulsory for employment as a teacher. One fifth of all the schools in Wales are Welsh medium schools, and some of the universities offer all their degree courses in the Welsh language too.

Without similar measures, the Sicilian language could really be lost one day. You would never see an official website written Sicilian. Even the Sicilians themselves would regard that as hilarious! The vast majority of Sicilians speak Sicilian the way my husband usually does – Italian with lots of Sicilian words poked in, and a few random Sicilian phrases, which of course is not really the Sicilian language at all. Most of them do not know how to speak pure Sicilian with all the correct grammar and exclusively Sicilian vocabulary. Only the fishermen in my village speak that way, and my husband says that, when they speak among themselves, he is unable to understand them.

There are some projects to protect the real Sicilian language. The European Union gives grants to help amateur theatre groups produce plays in Sicilian. That keeps the **piciotti** busy. They also organize other cultural activities such as poetry readings and musical performances which help to keep the language alive. Sicilian is spoken by communities in America, Argentina, Australia and other countries, yet Sicilian is not an official language anywhere, even within Sicily. There is currently no central body, in Sicily or elsewhere, that regulates the language in any way. However, the Center for Sicilian Philological and Linguistic Studies in Palermo has been researching and publishing information on the Sicilian language since it was founded in 1951.

I think they must still have a lot of work to do, for Sicilian is not just one language. There are so many different dialects, with their own unique vocabulary, that you only have to drive about one hour in any direction and you will find the local dialect is almost incomprehensible, sometimes even to a pretty good Sicilian speaker. My husband spent part of his military service years in Catania, and had no idea what anyone was saying the whole time they spoke in Sicilian.

One of the conversations I have had many a time arises when I hear a word I do not know.

"Is that a Sicilian or an Italian word?" I will ask, and then a general discussion ensues, which may draw in innocent bystanders at the supermarket or people who were passing by in the street. Nobody is sure. The huddle eventually disperses with a general agreement to look it up when they get home.

Many Sicilian words are unmistakably Sicilian though. There is nothing quite so colourful in Italian. This is part of the reason why Sicilians have the terribly irritating habit of starting a joke in Italian, and then delivering the punch line in Sicilian, which I usually cannot understand.

"It's just not funny in Italian" they say. And they are right.

They also use Sicilian when they are shamelessly spreading gossip. They lower their voices, lean into each other and mutter in Sicilian, making repeated use of personal pronouns instead of actual names, as they describe shocking and outrageous activities. If you hear lots of **idda** (she) or **iddu** (he) coming from the next room, it just might be you they are talking about.

Another situation in which Italian will often melt into Sicilian is an argument. When a forthright exchange of opinions descends into a knockdown verbal fight, it inevitably becomes a shouting match in Sicilian. Whilst the language lends itself more readily to wit, it also lends itself willingly to evocative insults and colourful threats. As both parties gradually run out of steam and come to the inevitable making up, which all Italian arguments always do eventually, the participants will revert to using Italian to show that they have regained their self-control.

It's almost a pity when that happens...

This will be enough to get us started

Sicilian housewives are scrubbers. Honestly. They spend more time scrubbing things than in any other activity, save possibly ironing.

When I worked in a bank in London, I thought that being able to sew would stand me in good stead when I became a housewife. I thought it meant I had *potential*. Then I met The Godmother, who is the very walking definition of uxoriousness in flesh and blood, and I realised how much more difficult it was all going to be than I had ever imagined.

For example, I had always thought – foolishly, as it now turns out – that there were certain objects in this world which it is simply never necessary to clean. Ever.

The pavement, for example, was something I had never once looked at in my life and thought, 'Well now, I think I'll give that a good scrub.' Yet, apparently, to be a decent housewife, a decent Sicilian one at any rate, it is essential to wash the pavement outside one's house quite regularly, on one's hands and knees, using a scrubbing brush that could flay an elephant and the kind of cleaning products that you probably need a special license to purchase in England.

Similarly, I had never once been tempted to lather up a set of iron railings and then rinse them down, dry them and buff them up with a soft cloth. I just figured that the rain took care of removing clumps of dirt, slattern that I was. Another item I imagined could be left unwashed throughout its whole existence was my wardrobe. I had spent years in England squirting it with Mr. Sheen and giving it a quick buff-up with a cloth to get the visible deposits of dust off it. Once I moved to Sicily, however, I was made to realise I had been leaving it to accumulate filth and that the only way a respectable housewife would treat such an item of furniture would be to wash it thoroughly with ammonia and water and then dry it with a series of special cloths, first a cotton one and then a woollen one and then one in microfibre.

One day, The Godmother came round to my house when I had just swept and mopped all the floors. She was wearing her black skirt and black blouse, which is what Sicilian housewives put on when they really mean business. She gave me a pitying, or perhaps critical, look and said,

"Oh, you poor thing! You must be so worn out with all this unpacking and organising that you haven't had time to clean the floor."

"Erm, yes," I said.

"Don't worry," she said, her nose already in the cleaning products cupboard she had given me as a house warming present. "I'll take care of it."

She extracted a thing which looked like a broom with no bristles and then wrapped it in a cloth which she dipped in something that smelled pungent enough to make my nose run, and proceeded to rub it all over the floor with so much verve I thought she might actually erode the glaze off the tiles.

"That's just given it a quick removal of the main dirt," she said, as she got on her knees and proceeded to pull the plinth away from the fitted cupboards under and around the kitchen sink.

She put the steel strips on the balcony and then proceeded to remove the entire underside of the island unit as well. Not satisfied with this, she then prised all the knobs off the hob, did something that looked downright painful to remove the oven door and then turned the extractor fan over the cooker into no less than eighteen separate, yet almost identical-looking, pieces of plastic grille.

Whilst I was profoundly shocked to see her calmly pull my kitchen to pieces, I was also flabbergasted that she was actually able to. For my whole life, up to that point, I had believed you needed men with exposed bum cleavages to do that type of thing.

While I was still searching for appropriate words, she filled the sink with several potent products, which foamed and gave off a greenish hallucinogenic vapour, and put all the small components of my ex-kitchen in it. While I sat down to regain some breath, she filled a bucket with whatever the Mafia use to dissolve dead bodies away to nothing except a few gold fillings, and started rubbing it into the pieces of stainless steel plinth she had yanked off the cupboards. I had chosen a matt finish but she kept working away at each piece of metal until she had made it look like a mirror.

I felt exhausted simply from watching all this manual labour, but I also began to realise I was suffering some kind of acute respiratory crisis. I was wheezing loudly and my vision was clouding over as if there were some type of jelly stuck to the front of my eyeballs. Apparently my eyes were turning maroon and I sounded like a Fiat that had accidentally been filled with diesel. I was having a severe allergic reaction to The Godmother's cleaning products.

I dashed into the bathroom and begged her to identify the pack of antihistamine I knew I had stashed away somewhere. She rummaged about and asked how many tablets I wanted. I told her to give me all of them. As I was shovelling them into my mouth, I realised she was buffing up the mirror with a dry cloth between popping the pills out of the foil blisters. She is the kind of woman who, if one of her children got his head stuck in a saucepan, would give it a jolly good polish before taking him to the hospital. If someone broke into her house by throwing a brick through the window she would wash the brick before calling the police. If she ever drank tea she would iron the teabags before using them.

Always read the label

I made my way out of the house, out of the chemical inferno which had once been my kitchen, sneaked into the lemon orchard behind the house, and sat on a patch of scratchy grass under a tree. It was still swelteringly hot but at least there was some shade which protected my watering eyes from the full power of the sunlight. I would like to say, especially if any minors are reading this, that overdosing on oral antihistamines and snorting kitchen de-scaler is a stupid and dangerous thing to do.

I felt as if I were drifting out of my body and wafting around among the leaves of the lemon trees in the form of a curly green waft of vaporised ammonia, carbolic acid and hydrogen peroxide. I think I hallucinated the bit where the lemons were talking to me about how they liked me wiping them clean with my eyeballs. I think the bit where I slumped against the trunk of a tree and slowly keeled over through lack of oxygen may have been real. The bit where The Godmother shouted 'Veronica, Veronica, wake up!' was definitely right here on planet earth, and it worked.

Eventually I recovered from this experience and came to an important realisation: I may be a Sicilian housewife now, but I shall continue housewifing in a very English way. I'll never manage to do it the way Sicilian women do. I salute them, and I give up. So please excuse me while I step over a thick smear of ketchup on my way to the kettle, because I need a cup of tea.

The Palermo Earthquake

I think I should talk about the earthquake we had in Palermo the other week.

On a Japanese scale, of course, it was not even worth mentioning – it was a mere 4.3 on the Richter scale. But it did happen. And it happened to me which, of course, makes it MASSIVELY important.

It occurred on a blissful morning when was very busy having a lie-in. It was on Friday 13th, so maybe I should have expected something bad to happen.

My husband had the day off work and had volunteered to do the school run. Our son is not exactly a morning person, so getting him ready to bundle off to school is most definitely hard work. Nagging him to eat his breakfast instead of just staring at it while telling you how hungry he is takes about a quarter of an hour. Dressing him (and getting a hernia from the exertion) is far less tiring than cajoling him to make the effort himself. I was delighted to lumber Hubby with the task.

Palermo 1918 - one of the biggest earthquakes
the city has suffered

He had just got back from dropping the little lad off at school when suddenly my bed began to vibrate. It was accompanied by a deep thundering sound coming from the bowels of the earth, which was then embellished by my wardrobe creaking in an "I'm-thinking-about-falling-apart" kind of way and, most alarming, a general sense of the house swaying. The swaying aspect of the experience was a little like being drunk, though of course not nearly as much fun.

After the vibrating had stopped, I sprang out of bed, ran in several directions at once and then started downstairs, shouting "Did you feel that?"

I met my husband halfway, dashing upstairs while shouting "Did you feel that?"

19

At this point, I was still vaguely hoping I might be authorised to slip back into bed and keep going with my lie-in. Apparently not.

"Get your clothes on quick!" I was instructed. "We've got to go and get Luca out of school".

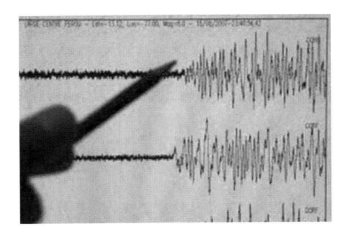

An earthquake being measured -
NOT the actual earthquake I was in (probably)

While I dressed in haste, my husband telephoned the school. He was told everything was fine and the children were not being sent home. We tuned into the news channel on TV to find out what was being reported, mainly worried that there may be further quakes.

I was reminded of my various English language students over the years from earthquake zones. I have several friends in Japan who suffered a great deal in the recent disaster that happened there. It was humbling to consider how alarmed we became as a result of a quake so tiny that, essentially, nothing happened whatsoever.

There was a very big earthquake in Sicily back in 2002 which measured 5.3 on the Richter scale and which damaged many historic buildings. It shook lots of plaster off the walls in some rooms of the stunningly beautiful Palazzo de Normanni in central Palermo, which dates from the eleventh century. Aftershocks continued for several weeks and everyone became very jittery. My husband's flat was filled with cracks, which he was fairly pleased about when he found he could get a government grant to have the whole place redecorated and re-plastered.

As in all serious situations, my mind was inevitably drawn to the ridiculous. I recalled a Turkish student who wrote me a composition in class, in which she described surviving a "very loud earthquack." I was also reduced to sniggering – as I always am - when I remembered a Georgian student whose pencil-written homework had been vandalized by his older brother before handing it in to me. His cruel brother had selectively erased letters, or parts thereof. Thus the essay I received recounted the terrifying experience of this teenaged boy's house partially falling down around his ears during the "biggest fart quake" of his life.

After half an hour of watching "earthquake in Palermo" reports on Sicilian TV, and chatting excitedly by telephone and text and internet with everyone else in Palermo, the school telephoned us.

"Can you come and get your son, please? The school has been evacuated."

When we arrived, it turned out that the school had been evacuated as soon as the earthquake happened, at the very same moment we had telephoned the school. This meant the little fellow had been waiting outside for us the entire time we were anxiously watching TV. He was blissfully happy.

"Guess what?" he greeted me. "My bag is in the class, so that means I can't do any homework!"

"They're not letting anyone inside again," his teacher explained apologetically.

"No school and no homework!" he shouted at the top of his voice as I led him to the car. "Earthquakes are fantastic! Do you think we'll have another one tomorrow?"

My washing machine caused the whole family great embarrassment this weekend. It has no excuse. It is still new!

The laundry I put into it looked fairly clean and just needed to be freshened up but, when it came out, it was coated all over in brownish-black stains which looked for all the world like the skid marks of someone with a serious bowel disease. The sight of my husband's underpants reduced to this condition gave me a very bad dream on Saturday night which I do not wish to describe.

This was a laundry disaster far worse than the time I shank all my jumpers into bare-midriff teenager-tops, or even the time I poured loo cleaner into the washing detergent drawer and bleached my husband's trousers to a very nasty shade of apricot. Whatever would the Godmother say?

Not knowing what else to do, I hung the damaged undies up to dry, intending to get a man to look at the machine before attempting to wash them again. Before I could do any such thing, however, the wind started blowing. Not any old wind, but the Scirocco; that hot, desiccating, merciless wind that blows up from the Sahara desert and makes you nearly suffocate. It turns the whole of Sicily into a tumble dryer.

When a broom from my balcony took off and flew over the treetops as if being ridden by an invisible witch, I decided it would be wise to go inside and shut all the windows. From my kitchen window vantage point I watched various packets of high-velocity washing powder and low-flying cleaning cloths hurtle past, and then the detached halves of clothes pegs, and then, some pieces of cloth which looked a lot like Hubby's underpants. I sidled across the room to check the washing line and they had, indeed, vanished... every last pair of them.

He eventually came back from work on his motorbike, almost flying like ET going home. He darted into the garage and told me about the various pieces of wood and plants he had seen flying around in the air on his way through Palermo. He seemed somewhat agitated, I would say. The wind blew for most of the night and was punctuated by extremely loud thumping and cracking noises echoing through the walls of our house, which eventually died down in the early hours of the morning.

I went outside very early the next day for a stroll to the supermarket, intending to replace the missing washing powder. The calm after the storm revealed scenes of devastation wherever I looked. Apart from the astounding number of cleaning products in bottles and handleless mops rolling about the place, there were former pieces of furniture, shattered roof tiles, long and structural-looking planks of wood, whole stiff sheets of roofing felt, and components of what I suppose were once bicycles and scooters.

Then suddenly, unexpectedly, there were Hubby's underpants, the whole gregarious flock of them sticking together loyally. They had draped themselves all over the trees in my neighbour's garden, like the gigantic cactus blooms that spring up in the desert once every seven years after a freak rainstorm and only last 24 hours. I stopped to gaze upon them in all their glory, while I inwardly contemplated the frailty of such flowers, and the ephemeral nature of our brief passage on this earth.

I nearly jumped out of my skin when my neighbour greeted me from behind a thick bush.

"What a storm!" she began. "Our garden furniture all blew away."

"Oh dear," I sympathised. "Yes, it was a very violent wind, wasn't it?"

"Did you lose anything?" she asked me.

I gazed upwards at the wondrous crop of "blooms" (bloomers?) which the night had brought to her garden. The indelible skid marks were all facing outwards, mucky-side-up, so to speak.

"No," I replied. "Nothing. I lost nothing at all."

Sicilian Driving Part 1: Correct Use of The Horn

I just peeled a bit more of my car off against another vehicle this morning. I am gradually working down in layers, whilst accumulating stripes of other cars' paint in every colour of the rainbow.

"Great! We found a parking space!"

In England, of course, we would call this an "accident". It would mean I had to stop, leave my insurance details and the car would be re-sprayed at considerable expense and irritation to the owner. In Sicily on the other hand, this is just regarded as 'normal wear and tear'. Many roads in our town are about ten to twelve feet wide, and when someone decides to park diagonally on the corner, they are clearly asking for their car to be turned into a rainbow.

Driving in Sicily is so much more advanced than driving in England that an English driving license could probably be regarded as an intermediate qualification, a sort of "proof of fitness" that one is ready to become a learner driver in Sicily.

I shall now share some tips for anyone thinking of visiting this madhouse of an island. One essential habit for surviving driving in Sicily is the same as the key habit to make a marriage work: constant communication. When in a car, you communicate with other road users using the horn. It is used for friendly greetings, telling other drivers what you intend to do (so much more practical than the indicators, which are usually broken anyway) and for telling other drivers what they should do.

Any time you see a car appearing in a side road, give one sharp hoot on your car horn. If you fail to do this, they will assume you are inviting them to pull out in front of you, and will do so even if you are at a distance of ten centimetres from them and travelling at three hundred miles per hour. The friendly little toot tells them: "My foot is on the accelerator, and it is staying there."

When you see someone you know, deliver two greeting hoots if you have no sense of rhythm, or else tap out a little tune if you are musically inclined. You could hoot along to the dance music you are listening to and wave a little hand jive to them as well. I believe some extremely advanced drivers actually use Morse Code.

Be sure to stop and talk to them for a few minutes, but remember that road placement is essential in this situation. You must position your car precisely in the middle of the road so that no other vehicle travelling in either direction is able to pass until you have finished chatting. The driver of one of the vehicles just might be a mutual friend and it would be a tragedy if he were to drive on by and miss the opportunity to join in the conversation.

Mild wear and tear
but nothing noticeable

If you find yourself stuck in a traffic jam, you must hoot your horn incessantly for the full two or more hour duration of the blockage. It is vital! You *must* do your part to help clear whatever is causing the delay. Your contribution DOES count. If everyone joins in intelligently hooting together, you CAN make a difference.

Another important use of the horn is using it to draw other drivers out of shops. Sicilians often lament the fact that they are highly strung and fly off the handle at the drop of a hat, wishing they had more of what they call our "Anglo-Saxon self-control". Yet I am continually astounded at the phlegm they display when finding their car boxed in by a mêlée of about twenty vehicles.

A few scratches
but otherwise in perfect condition

If someone found themselves boxed in by a double-parker in England, they would probably call the police without waiting ten seconds. Sicilians will patiently sit in their car, or stand near it, giving the occasional laid-back hoot on the horn for simply ages, waiting for the owners of the other vehicles to amble out of the bank, pharmacy or some other establishment. Then everyone rearranges their cars to let one out, double and triple parking them again, and slowly dispersing back into the various shops they were perusing.

It is essential to hoot at any car as you overtake it. Otherwise it may swerve suddenly and unpredictably into you, leading to a side impact which could drive you off the road. Under such circumstances the driver is normally avoiding a cluster of run-over dogs or cats. (Once there is one dead feline in the road, others cannot resist sniffing their decomposing companion as part of the mourning process, thus terminating their own lives prematurely and creating the phenomenon of dead cat 'art installations'.) Alternatively, he may be avoiding a pile of broken glass and some vehicle components shed in an earlier accident. Certainly do not expect the driver to look out for you in his rear view mirror before dealing with these obstacles. That mirror is for him to hang his rosary beads and picture of Saint Rosalia off.

N.B. Rear view mirror religious artefacts are indispensable for safe driving in Italy, and will be dealt with in a separate tutorial.

The final use of the horn in Italy might perhaps be the most famous: celebration. When you happen to win the World Cup, or your team wins any significant football tournament, you must celebrate by forming a slow-moving cavalcade of cars, scooters and motorbikes, all hooting your horns continuously throughout the night. Drive by everyone's house to ensure they are all awake. Keep going till the car battery is flat, then push the car home.

So there you have it, *part one* of Driving in Sicily. Don't miss the next instalment: **Correct use of indicators and hazard lights for decoration, greeting, and illegal parking.**

Inspiration at the Supermarket

I pootled off to the village supermarket today. There is really nothing very super about the local supermarket. I rarely go there, but today I was feeling too ill to manage anything further afield.

My village is not exactly a frenzy of commercial enterprise. Besides the supermarket, it contains a baker's, an ice-cream shop, a barber, a ladies' hairdresser, a hardware shop, a purveyor of rotten meat, five cafés and a post office full of violent old age pensioners fighting each other to the service hatch.

Occasionally other shops spring up briefly, but then go out of business after a year or so. That is because of those people we don't like to talk about, demanding too much *pizzo* or extortion money, so that the shopkeeper cannot make ends meet. When shops go out of business in this way, the owners tend not to say why. They tell you they simply decided to turn their hand to other activities. Only if they know and trust you do they confide the real reason – because blabbing about such events to the wrong people could put them in further danger.

In the supermarket, they had changed everything. Has it really been so long since I last went there? I went looking for urgent supplies of tea, though I should have known better. Eventually I found myself in an aisle with a pasta section, in which all the bags of pasta were simply enormous sacks. There was no packet smaller than a pillowcase, and they were all on the upper shelves. Stacked below them, rather off-puttingly, were cans of dog food. This was the pasta for dogs. Oh yes! Pasta for dogs. In Italy, you can buy your canine friend fusilli, tortellini or almost any other shape of pasta he may have acquired a taste for, and then add a sauce of chummed up Pedigree Chum, or whatever.

Pedigree Pasta? Spillers Choice Spaghetti?

The concept of dedicated dog pasta no longer takes me by surprise. After eight years in Sicily, very little takes me by surprise, actually. My husband used to lovingly warm up leftover pasta to give to his now deceased dog, Leo. He kept a supposedly fierce guard dog at his grandmother's house, supposedly to protect her. I am making generous use of the word "supposedly" because the dog was in fact more timid than a sparrow, and would hide under the bed at the first sign of a postman. Personally I attribute this to being abnormally pampered in every way, starting with food.

Dogs are supposed to munch up leftovers without complaint, whatever they may be. That is why we sigh and say "Ah, it's a dog's life." That is the canine condition. It is the very nature of dogginess.

But not Leo. The Hubby would stand at the stove lovingly warming up leftover pasta for Leo, tasting it and adding a pinch more salt or a touch of fresh basil if he felt its flavour needed improving, and checking that it was the ideal temperature by dabbing some onto his inner wrist, like testing milk for a baby, before finally serving it up for Leo in the garden. He often served it with a side-dish of salad, or some parsley garnish. I am convinced that sometimes, when he wandered into the garden with a glass of red wine in his hand, it was actually an aperitif for Leo. If he felt that Leo may be suffering from poor digestion or trapped wind he massaged his tummy. After dinner he often gave him an After Eight mint.

Moving hastily away from the dog food section, I located the miserable offerings on sale by way of compensation for the lack of actual tea in Italy. The very lowest standard of teabags are the only sort commercially available in Sicily. They contain no tea at all, just the sweepings of dust, small twigs and maybe a few crushed cockroach carapaces from the tea-factory floor. To this they add crumbled gerbil poos to add bulk and enrich the colour.

A gerbil, Italian Tea Breed

The thing that bothers me about these teabags even more is the fact that they are on strings. Teabags are not supposed to be on strings. Tampons are supposed to be on strings. I shall say no more.

I loaded about twelve packets into my trolley, calculating that, since you have to use six such "tea" bags per cup to get any flavour whatsoever, this would last me about four days. I resolved to renew my periodic attempts to acquire a taste for coffee as soon as possible.

The human pasta section in Italian supermarkets - including this one - occupies both sides of two full aisles, even in a supermarket with no more than ten aisles altogether. This aisle is magnificently impressive and often makes me lose all sense of time. I spent ages looking at the names of each pasta shape and thinking about what they actually mean. Every pasta shape has a name which is highly descriptive and apt. Farfalle are butterflies, spaghetti are short bits of string, vermicelli are little worms, linguine are little tongues, conchiglie are shells, gomiti are elbows, orechiette are little ears, lumache are snails, and ravioli are little frilly cushions stuffed with vomit. I confess I am not absolutely certain about the translation of that last one, but I think it means something like that.

Like all normal Italians, my husband is utterly convinced that failing to eat any pasta during one continuous 24-hour period means certain death. To avoid such danger, I loaded one bag of almost every pasta shape I could find into my trolley, plus four packs of spaghetti for good measure.

I went rather wild at the cheese and delicatessen counter, buying a vast selection of expensive smoked Sicilian cheeses, costly smoked hams and high-end mortadella. I also suddenly realized that we desperately need some stuffed olives dressed with fresh herbs; we were completely out of marinated artichoke hearts; I could not possibly go home without a reasonable supply of porcini mushrooms in olive oil; and I was astonished when I realised that we did not even have staples like salmon paté or smoked swordfish at home.

I am afraid I always do this when I go to the supermarket, which is probably why my husband so often volunteers to go for me. Everything is displayed so temptingly and sounds so appealing.

Frankly, a lot of Italian food is the same as English food but, somehow, the Italians just do it better. Mortadella is a good example because it is actually spam. The only difference is that spam tastes like what it is, namely, a pig's snout, lips and earlobes blended with a little bit of its backside, whereas mortadella tastes like a fabulous delicacy because it also has garlic, pistachio nuts and an Italian name.

The Italian Christmas Panettone is really nothing more than a giant-sized loaf of raisin bread. Even pizza, if you think about it, is just a glorified version of cheese on toast. It is all a question of presentation. Another great Italian marketing triumph is minestrone soup which, as we all know, is ketchup with some leftover vegetables and pasta tipped in.

The all-time greatest Italian makeover story has to be, of course, Parmesan cheese. This is no more than ordinary cheese that got left in the larder three generations ago and was rediscovered in a partially mummified condition, grated to look like dandruff, and then sold in automatically reloading sprinkler devices so that Italian waiters could use it for getting revenge on women who rejected the suggestive advances they made with their massive phallic black pepper dispensers.

Happy with my selection of items, apart from the tea of course, I tottered off to the till with my trolley which, its gammy wheels weighed down with pasta, was determined to roll off sideways into the sunset. The strangest thing about the village supermarket is the woman who works on the till. She is the real reason I like going to this supermarket.

She is always there, and there is only one till. I have never seen anyone else capable of looking so close to death, for such a prolonged period of time, without actually dying. Her name is Angela, but I think of her as Vampire Angela. Her face is a translucent blueish white, her eyes are hollow and sad and the exhaustion on her face is so profound that even her whitish-grey hair looks as if it is too tired to keep holding onto her scalp for much longer. The cadaverous look is enhanced when she smiles and reveals teeth that look dry and loose in their sockets. Yet she keeps on going, day after week after month, just the same, and she always says she is fine every time I see her. In this village we see everyone all over the place. It is too small not to. Yet I have never seen Vampire Angela anywhere except in the supermarket, sitting at the till, looking whiter and greyer every time I lay eyes on her.

When I got home with my loot, I made myself a nice hot, steaming urea-coloured gerbil dung infusion and thought about Angela. I think she is braver than me. She has no idea of it, and I don't know her well enough to say so, but she is my role model. And that, friends, is why I like this supermarket.

When I started this blog I decided I was not going to mention illness at all, but the fact is, I have a heart condition and, frankly, I sometimes feel awful. And yet... Angela looks, and clearly feels, so much worse than I do, yet she keeps on going, she never gives up, and she always says she is fine.

Her stoical suffering inspires me.

Sicilian Medicine... or is it Magic?

I nearly got run over after dropping my son off at school this week. As it turned out, the driver swerved in the nick of time, swore in Sicilian, and drove off. So essentially, nothing actually happened. Yet I was left in a state of utter agitation.

Instead of going straight home, I decided to drop in on a friend in the village, in order to let off steam by gibbering at her.

She was having breakfast sitting just inside her front door - which meant she was in the middle of her kitchen - having a shouted chat with the neighbour across the road, who happened to be sitting in *her* kitchen, drinking coffee. Despite both being in their separate homes, they were not fifteen feet from each other, having breakfast together.

"I knew something was wrong," my friend said. "You're so pale and wiped out. You've got worms. I could see it."

"What did you say?" I asked, assuming I had misunderstood.

"You've got worms," she repeated, slowly.

"I definitely haven't," I said. "I just had a scare."

She laughed like a drain. "That's what I mean," she said. "In Sicilian, we say you've got worms if you've had a big scare and you can't calm down afterwards. It feels as if you've got worms in your tummy, creeping around and keeping you agitated. I'll do the prayer to heal the worms for you. It's our thing, a kind of magic medicine."

A prayer? To heal metaphorical worms?

I agreed, purely because I was curious to find out what this "prayer" would be like.

She stood up and solemnly closed the door. The lady across the road gave an understanding look, and glanced at me encouragingly. I was receiving medical treatment. Neighbours were not allowed to watch.

My newly self-appointed witch doctor poured some olive oil onto a plate and made me stand near it, by the table. She lifted up my top to expose my bare tummy, and told me to close my eyes and try to think only of the olive oil. Then she dipped her thumb into the oil, closed her eyes, and started to make a very tiny sign of the cross in the oil on my tummy, over and over again, while muttering a rhythmic poem too quietly for me to hear.

Maybe it was the rubbing, which was quite relaxing. Maybe her voice was very soothing. Maybe the prayer really did have power and maybe olive oil actually does have magical properties. But it worked. I actually felt perfectly calm at the end of it, serene even. The worms were gone.

She told me that the magic of the prayer can only be passed on to another person on Christmas Eve, at midnight. You teach the prayer to the person you have chosen to share it with, and they have to memorise it there and then. It must never be written down, and it must never be revealed to another person except in this way. If the person you have passed on the magic to casually reveals any part of the secret, not only do they lose the ability to do the magic, but so do you.

I spoke to my husband about this afterwards. He told me he once had sunstroke as a child. His mother, The Godmother, frog-marched him off to an

31

old woman who lived nearby for "treatment". The treatment for sunstroke involved having the plate of olive oil balanced on your head, and a piece of cotton wool soaked in it, then set alight. After saying an inaudible prayer, the woman clapped a cup over the cotton wool to put out the fire.

He said he did feel somewhat better after this ritual, but he suspected that was at least in part owing to relief that his hair had not been set alight. Also, The Godmother, never one to take chances, also stuffed him full of aspirin, water, sugar and salt, orange juice, and any other potential treatment she could think of.

Olives and their oil have been central to all Mediterranean and Middle Eastern cultures for many thousands of years. Olive oil is packed with nutritious substances and it is literally impossible for bacteria to grow in it, so it became a central part of medicine in ancient times as it genuinely can disinfect many types of infection. Its cleansing qualities made it ideal for washing, in place of soap, and made it take on a role in ritual purifications. Some oil was made specifically for medicinal purposes, and was pressed from bitter olives, either unripe ones or wild ones which taste far too awful to eat. The oil was the mainstay of many economies, such a source of wealth that it was used to anoint Kings. Oil that had gone rancid was never thrown away, but burnt in oil lamps to make light after the sun went down, and for this reason became part of many sacred rituals performed in dark, gloomy temples. Olive oil is still the only oil allowed to be used in certain sacred rites in the Jewish, Christian and Muslim faiths. Perhaps I have been privy to a prayer used for several thousands of years?

While I am talking about olive oil, do let me tell you why you should always buy extra virgin olive oil. I know I am pontificating here. Well, why not? I'm good at it, aren't it?

To qualify as extra virgin, the oil has to be less than 1% acid. The achieve this, the olives need to receive the kid-glove treatment from start to finish. They have to be picked by hand, as mechanical pickers would bruise them, triggering the oxidification process which makes them become acidic. Picking them by hand means going up ladders and agitating tree branches to make the olives fall onto clean white sheets carefully laid out on the ground. Every Sicilian, who can afford to, keeps a smallholding in the country to grow their own olives, and ropes in all their relatives to help at olive picking time, which is November.

Once you have started picking your olives, you have to finish as soon as possible and get them to the *frantoio*, the oil press, immediately. If they sit about for a few days they will start to oxidize and go acid. At the *frantoio* they are crushed mechanically between stone wheels. The pulp is spread onto thin mats which are stacked in a stainless steel press. As pressure is applied, oil and water-based juice seep out. No heat is used, so this oil is called "first cold pressed."

After pressing, water and oil are separated. People who have taken their own crop of olives to the *frantoio* usually take it home like this, with the sediment still in it, as this imparts fantastic flavor. Oil made for commercial use has the sediment filtered out, as this gives it a longer shelf life, which is why the stuff you can buy in supermarkets is always filtered. Olive oil, once pressed, lasts about 18 months before going rancid.

Extra-virgin olive oil is required by law to have no more than 1% percent acidity (less than 1% free oleic acid), which makes it much healthier than virgin olive oil (2% or less acidity) and pure olive oil (higher than 2% acidity).

When olives are picked mechanically or bruised before they are pressed, or when the olive oil oxidizes, acidity levels increase. Therefore, lower acidity is an indication of better quality. Oils that are found to be too acidic after the first pressing are sent to a refinery, where color, taste and aroma are altered by industrial processing. Chemicals are used, and the oil becomes colorless and tasteless and loses its distinct character; this inferior oil can then be blended with some virgin olive oil (which provides color and flavor) and then sold as "pure" olive oil. "Light" and "mild" olive oils are also made this way, using chemical processes and solvents, but less "virgin" oil is added to rectify flavor and color.

I have a friend who used to work in a *frantoio*. Strictly speaking, she not simply a friend, but I am saying that out of laziness. To be honest, she is my husband's sister's husband's brother's wife. I think that means she is my sister-in-law-in-law-in-law. Of course, in England you would never get to meet someone so tenuously connected to you, but in Sicily you spend Christmas and Easter and birthdays with them and stay in their houses for entire weekends, along with 35 other relatives so bizarrely connected that you don't know what to call them. (This, by the way, is the reason why Italians all seem to have about 3,000 cousins. They call everyone a cousin as they do not know what else to call them).

Anyway, my sister-in-law-in-law-in-law had to give up working in the *frantoio* as she developed a serious allergy to all types of olive oil other than extra virgin. She said, when they heat the oil it gives off a vapour that smells appalling and coats every part of you, so you are greasy and stinky. She said they also use hydrochloric acid to clean the machinery and the floor of the *frantoio*, otherwise you would be slipping over in grease as you walk about; drops of it constantly contaminate the oil but nobody cares. If she eats any grade of oil that has been processed or heated, or indeed extra virgin oil that has been cooked with, she swells up like the Michelin man and struggles to breathe. Yet raw, pure extra virgin olive oil has no effect on her at all.

I wonder if there is an olive oil prayer that could cure her.

A Recipe: Fresh citrus fruit cakes

There's only one cake left now...

The other day I baked a stonkingly delicious batch of Sicilian cakes flavoured with fresh citrus fruit from the neighbour's orchard opposite our house.

Oh alright, maybe I have exaggerated a teensy bit. Actually, I watched my husband bake them. But so what? I still know how to make them.

Besides, working by proxy is a great Sicilian tradition. Whenever you see a Sicilian man working in a hole in the road, there are at least twelve others standing around watching him, and providing constructive criticism to egg him on. I like to help my husband cook in a similar fashion.

It all started when the hubby came home bearing a wooden crate of about 250 oranges. Events like this are absolutely commonplace in Sicily, where citrus trees grow like weeds. Lemon trees bear fruit literally all year round, but oranges appear in December and keep growing abundantly through till late March, along with their cousins the mandarins and tangerines. They are so sweet and juicy and so freely available that everyone indulges in an orgy of juice drinking, jam making and any other form of citrus-based gluttony they can dream up.

My husband's one's bigger than this

When you walk into a bar in Sicily and order an orange juice, the barman will stand and squeeze oranges in front of you, usually by hand, one after another till he has filled up a glass. The excitement mounts, your taste buds get activated, and you have to make efforts to avoid drooling onto the bar as the glass gradually fills. Sicilians seem to have such a skillful way of juicing oranges! They must grow up with a lifetime of orange squeezing, and have citrus fruit in their blood. There is something about watching the juice squeezed by a maestro that makes it all the more delicious when you drink it.

One of my favourite Sicilian snacks is citrus cakes. The proper Sicilian way to eat them is for breakfast, with a glass of freshly squeezed orange juice and a milky coffee. They are also divine eaten the English way, at teatime with a nice pot of PG Tips. If you're interested in getting really fat, you can slice them horizontally and fill them with a dollop of clotted cream.

The cakes are dairy free, and work beautifully if made with gluten free flour.

Here's the recipe:

INGREDIENTS

600 grammes / 21 oz of flour (normal or gluten free – if using gluten free, pure potato flour is the nicest)

200 grammes / 7 oz sugar

180 ml / 6 fl oz of freshly squeezed orange juice

150 ml / 5 fl oz of maize oil (other vegetable oils are OK)

Finely grated zest of 1 or 2 organic, unwaxed oranges (one for mild flavor, two for a strong taste; you can use one orange and one lemon instead if you like)

3 eggs

One very heaped teaspoon of baking powder

ALSO

About 20 paper cases for cupcakes

Icing sugar to dust on top

METHOD

1. Put all the ingredients in your blender and whizz for 2 minutes. (Ah! Don't you just love recipes like this?) You can use an electric whisk if you have no blender.

2. Half fill all the paper cases with the mix.

3. Bake in a preheated oven at 190 degrees centigrade for 25 minutes, then turn off the oven and leave the cakes inside or another 5 minutes before removing them.

4. Use your tea-strainer to dust the tops with icing sugar.

Whilst I am on the subject of citrus fruit, I would like to impart some important information about orange juice. Sicily is so awash with oranges that it is easy to meet people who work in the orange juice industry, and thus learn insider information.

Do you ever buy orange juice in cartons, which says somewhere in tiny writing "orange juice *made from concentrate*"? Have you ever wondered why it tastes a bit yucky compared to juice you have just squeezed yourself?

The answer is that this juice also contains the orange zest. In the industry, these blocks of frozen oil from the peel are called "flavour packs". This oil has a similar flavour to the juice inside the orange, once you add enough sugar and water, but it is also very bitter and this cannot be disguised. It is fully legal not to declare this on the packaging. Would you buy a carton of juice labeled "Orange juice *made from peel*?"

Oh, you've got a cold? Drink a glass of pith.
That'll make you feel better.

About five fresh oranges would be needed to fill a modest glass with juice; yet if you use the zest, one single orange could fill five or six such glasses. By the time you factor in the costs of transporting tiny containers of concentrated zest, compared to litres of juice, you can begin to see the economic appeal.

One thing manufacturers tend to do to this juice made from "concentrate" is to add vitamin C. This is presumably because they feel guilty selling a carton of so-called orange juice that contains hardly any natural vitamin C. Another reason is that the ascorbic acid acts as a preservative and also helps the drink taste more like real juice.

Eating orange zest is not bad for you. I not only put it in cakes, but also coarsely grate it into the teapot with some normal tea to make an orange tea, which I find far nicer than Early Grey or other flavoured teas. You can put grated lemon or orange zest into small bottles of olive oil to create your own fabulous salad oils. You can stir it into a jar of runny honey to create a flavoured honey for breakfast, or for sweetening tea. Making your own marmalade is also easy and turns out far more delicious than any shop marmalade I have ever tasted; citrus pith is crammed with pectin, so literally all you need is the fruit, and the same weight in sugar.

Just make sure you are always using organic oranges when you do this, and soak them in water for plenty of time before you use them. If you decide to grate the zest of an orange but do not need the juice yet, wrap it in foil in the fridge to stop it drying out.

The man from Del Monte, He say, CONCENTRATE!

Well, I am off now to have some fresh orange juice. Not made from concentrate.

Bottoms up!

Sicilian Fashion and How to Emulate It

The other day I went out shopping for clothes in the local town, Bagheria. Bagheria is full of shops and about 80 percent of them are clothes shops. The other 20 percent are shoe shops. One could be forgiven, therefore, for assuming that my mission was easy. Wrong! Buying wearable clothes in Sicily is almost as difficult as detaching Luciano Pavarotti from a ricotta-filled cannoli.

Forget Italian style and elegance. That has not crossed the little strip of sea separating Sicily from the continent. The fact is, they have fashions here that never have existed, and never will exist, anywhere else in the world. Some memorable examples I have witnessed over the years include tartan hipster Bermuda shorts worn with fishnets underneath and plastic stilettos (Summer 2008); gold and silver trainers for all ages and both sexes (2008 to 2010); and everywhere, on everyone, spectacularly skin tight T-shirts with bizarre slogans written on them in incorrect English (forever).

The first shop I passed was one of the many owned by Chinese immigrants. We have growing armies of them in Sicily nowadays. The Chinese triads have an arrangement with the Sicilian Mafia which involves importing illegal immigrants, and defective goods for them to sell, which would not pass any EU safety regulation whatsoever. They nearly always offer clothing, dyed with toxic chemicals which smell of naphthalene and diesel oil and which may make you infertile, hallucinate or lose your epidermis.

I was unable to resist the temptation to pop into the shop, just to see what it would be like. Mostly it contained footwear with six inch heels thinner than pencils. The assistant was a paunchy, middle aged man who spoke Cantonese and a little Sicilian, wearing a purple t-shirt bearing the unforgettable legend, "mysterious seducer." He was selling a pair of golden trainers to an elderly lady in a Lycra top with a picture of Tweetie Pie in sequins, and the words "This year I always am full of kiss" embroidered alongside. In my haste to escape I almost bumped into a round-shouldered granny using a Zimmer frame, sporting a tracksuit with "First world sexy sequin girl" written across the back in very shiny metallic letters.

The next shop I tried looked fairly promising from the window display, yet I was greeted by a sales assistant whose sartorial presentation disappointed. He wore a tracksuit with the unforgettable legend "UPPERCUT SCHOOL OF BOING" on the back. Whatever could that mean? My mind was flooded with wondrous images of prize athletes holding kick-boxing tournaments on trampolines. Or might Jackie Chan have invented a new martial art? Kung Fu performed upside down while bungee jumping?

The thing that makes this eternal fashion particularly annoying is that people constantly ask me to translate their outfits for them, and then look sceptical when I do. How could my beautiful, shiny T-shirt possibly say such drivel? I can see them thinking. They evidently splash out on these atrocious fashion blunders believing they are investing in quotations of philosophical wisdom, machine washable at 30 degrees centigrade.

I decided to take a short coffee break at a pavement café and sat pondering this passion for incorrect English. Pavement cafés are paradise for people like me, who love to make critical appraisals of their fellow men, undetected. I put on my Mafia-Black shades, and went to work. I should probably explain here that my Mafia sunglasses are magic spy glasses. To me, they are actually more exciting than X-ray specs. I do not know how this works, but whenever I look at someone with dyed hair through them, it makes it glow luminous red, just like a radioactive tomato. I do not know what type of radiation is emitted by hair dye, or how my specs filter and concentrate it. I think this may be because they are prescription sunglasses with lenses that I ordered from the cheapest optician in Western Europe. No matter. They make people-watching supremely entertaining.

Some residents of Bagheria manage to inspire fear and amazement simply by wearing a hostile expression and stubble you could use for striking matches. Other vintage specimens have missing teeth and ragged hair. The scariest of all, however, are those who use cutting edge fashion as their weapon.

I spotted a woman who could not have been under eighty years of age and ninety kilogrammes of weight in a Barbie pink velour tracksuit, like the ones Britney Spears wears when she is fat. I think everyone in the world knows that old Sicilian ladies are supposed to wear black dresses and shoes with bunion-shaped curves on the inner rim. When threatened, they can twirl rosary beads the way Bruce Lee brandished nunchakus. They do not need to use decoy tactics as well, such as disguising themselves as Hollywood starlets having drug-related psychological meltdowns. I slid my glasses down my nose to have a good look at her as she crept past, gazing in awe at her lilac sequinned bag, clutched in hands ravaged by arthritis.

Refreshed by caffeine, I returned to my shopping venture. I reached my favourite shop, which offers the best selection of wearable clothes in Bagheria. It is one of the "small size" shops.

Italian clothing shops come in two types: those which stock supposedly normal clothes, which are actually for anorexic midgets; and those which stock all the other sizes, considered "outsize" shops. To give you an idea of what I mean by anorexic midgets, let me explain that my favourite Bagherian clothes shop has four sizes, S, M, L and XL. In this shop I am size XL, which equates to a British dress size 12, which is an American size 8. Call me delusional, but frankly I do not think this is particularly large. That is why I think this shop is principally for anorexic midgets.

This might makes sense if Sicilians were actually midgets but, oh my goodness me, they are NOT! They eat far too many Fried spleen sandwiches to be small. Sicily is, after all, the place that invented the use of potato chips (that's French Fries to you Yanks) as a pizza topping.

This discrepancy between the size of the clothing and the size of the population means Sicilian women have to adopt one of two strategies. Some of them insert themselves into clothes five sizes too small and wear them proudly (until the seams burst), happy that they are trendy and that their jeans also double up as a corset. Those who are too voluptuous, or "prosperous," as the Italians call it, instead have to go to the outsize clothing shops, which Italians rather coyly call "comfortable sizes". For the larger gentlemen, by the way, outsize clothing is described as "strong sizes."

Those who resort to "comfortable" sizes are restricted to the truly desperate. Sicily is the only place in Europe where I have seen people who are super fat, American-fat, the sort who can no longer make their hands meet at the front of their tummy. So even these people wear their clothes perilously tight, putting the tensile strength of machine stitches to their ultimate test.

Just as a curious aside, I would like to mention that one of the stalls in Bagheria's Wednesday market has on sale a pair of trousers in such a strong size that you could actually prop them up on sticks and hold a complete circus performance inside them. Among friends and family who come to visit me in my luxurious Mediterranean home, these trousers with their kilometric waistband and balloon seat have become a well-known tourist attraction. I shall be devastated if anyone ever buys them.

The single most terrifying fashion blunder committed by almost the entire female population of Bagheria is the bare midriff. Despite the fact that they have passed into fashion history in the rest of the world, hipster jeans are NEVER going out of fashion here in Sicily. It is impossible to buy any trousers, anywhere in Sicily, with a waistband that reaches anywhere near your waist.

The bare midriff concept, I should hardly need to point out, was conceived as a means of displaying a tantalisingly sexy flash of bare skin on a slim, shapely girl. It has been reinterpreted in Bagheria. Here, it is regarded as an outlet, a sort of emergency pressure-valve to release surplus stones (or tons) of blubber when over-eating has reached such perilous proportions that the hipster jeans are groaning at every stitch, the muffin-top has flopped down so far under its unsustainable weight that the waistband is completely concealed, and the T-shirt is simply unable to expand any further widthways around the newly enlarged girth, so it suddenly snaps upwards and settles, in a ruched format, inside the dark, damp groove between the uppermost roll of belly fat and the monumentally sized bosoms. The number of breath-taking, heart-stopping, jaw-dropping teenage girls to be seen waddling around Bagheria and bouncing against the lampposts in this condition is, in my opinion, a contributing factor to the record-breaking number of traffic accidents occurring each year.

The need for anoraks is probably my favourite aspect of winter in Sicily.

Anyway, getting back on topic, I entered my favourite shop and discovered that, because of the economic crisis, they still had sale items left from January. I found an extra-large, comfortable sized cable-knit sweater dress which will do me just fine as a jumper. It looks great, it fits perfectly, and it only cost 6 Euros. Mission accomplished!

Sicilian driving part 2: Correct use of indicators and hazard lights for decoration, greeting, and illegal parking

I criticised the Sicilian department of transport in a comment on my previous post. They have reacted by increasing productivity

My car indicator is malfunctioning. I'm not worried. They are not very important in Sicily. And anyway, Fiat indicators tend to go on strike from time to time. They always start working again eventually, usually after a heavy rainfall.

However, this event is of course very topical, as it reminds me it's time for part two my "Driving in Sicily" online tutorial.

In Sicily, the first thing to learn is that you can't use the indicator willy-nilly.

You need to learn judicious use of those flashing orange lights. The idea is not to give away any information which could give the other driver the advantage. A classic beginner's mistake is to loiter near a parking space with the lights flashing. This alerts everyone in the neighbourhood to the fact that there's a parking space available and, of course, they'll devise means of getting into it before you do which your simple, innocent mind could never conceive of.

While on this subject I must warn you that you should never, ever, I repeat *ever*, pause to let a car out from a side road or parking space in front of you. The driver will consider you weak and possibly of a mentally unstable condition, and he'll warn other drivers about you. Absolutely nobody will ever thank you at all for your considerate behaviour, and eventually there's a danger you may become bitter and twisted and develop wrinkled brow lines.

Never use it when you're trying to pull into a stream of moving traffic. Why on earth would you warn anyone that you intend to pull in front of them, cut them up completely and then never actually get above fifteen kilometres an hour because your granny in the back gets scared? Those are the kind of drivers who indicate to pull out. If you do that, you'll instantly find that every car passing you is no more than three centimetres from the car in front of it.

41

When you get into the outside lane of a motorway or state road, you must activate your left hand indicator until you intend to cut in on someone. The indicator serves to let them know you're not intending to pull in yet, so they can safely overtake you on the inside.

This traffic lights tree stands on a
ROUNDABOUT in London's Docklands.
Was it a gift from the
Sicilian Department of Transport?

Sometimes the indicator is not used, simply because the complexity of a driving manoeuvre makes it impossible to decide whether the left or right indicator is appropriate. For example, suppose you decide to drive at 180 kph up the wrong side of the road, and then cut sharply across the path of another car to turn the corner while he performs an emergency stop. Should you indicate left to let people know you are pulling onto the wrong side of the road, or right, as your ultimate intention is to turn right? It's better simply to use the horn abundantly and also turn up your car stereo as loud as possible while performing this manoeuvre, to make sure everyone knows where you are and keeps out of your way. You could even hit the hazard light button too, if you want to be extra cautious. That way, you'll have both your left and your right indicators flashing, so all eventualities are covered

On the subject of hazard lights, please note that it is mandatory to turn them on whenever you are parked dangerously in a strictly no parking zone, such as blocking the entrance to an ambulance bay. The hazard lights tell people you are only there briefly and for a critically important purpose, such as to get some coffee in a nearby bar or to grab a quick deep-fried spleen sandwich.

Such use of the hazard lights has become standard in England and other countries too nowadays, so perhaps it was too obvious for me to mention. What do you think?

Spring is Springing, Wrinkles are Forming

Fishermen's boats on the beach in my village

Here in Sicily, spring is Springing. The sun is shining, the birds are tweeting, and the pollen is billowing about in allergenic clouds. It's March, and HEAT is approaching.

This has naturally got me thinking about sunscreen and wrinkles. In Sicily, you have to make a direct choice between one or the other. To stay white, or to go brown? To apply cream, or to become creviced? That is the question.

In England these days, the government's panic-mongering warnings about skin cancer have apparently made people forget the meteorological reality that the sun only shines in England about three times a year, weakly. People slather on sunscreen every time the cloud cover clears for a couple of hours. Many schools enforce a rule that sunscreen must be worn by all children at playtime, every day.

When I first moved to Sicily I had succumbed to the brainwashing, and smothered myself daily with SPF 50. I walked about looking like a Geisha. I was not tanning at all: My face was absorbing the rays of the sun merely in order to re-release them at dusk, making me phosphoresce. Confused moths fluttered around me in circles, I frightened the local fishermen, and the thick layer of grease permanently on my face made me re-live my teen years by sporting a steady crop of pimples.

Meanwhile back home in England, the newly seminated sunshine phobia was starting an epidemic of rickets among children. Southampton hospital found 20% of the children it tested had rickets, according to a BBC report. The same problem has spread nationwide. This government-inspired choice to become a nation deficient in vitamin D means that, beyond bone deformity, the

British are setting their children up for immune deficiency, increased risk of allergies, and obesity.

One of the village beaches where I frequently get sunburnt

There would be no risk of that for the Sicilians. Not only because the sun beats so hard you probably get 20 times the RDA of vitamin D every time you look out of the window, but also because the Sicilians dedicate their lives, from March to October, to getting tanned as leather-brown as they possibly can.

If you raise the topic of skin damage, they laugh heartily. "I've got Sicilian skin!" They say. "It's tougher than cow hide!"

You would never catch a Sicilian sporting geisha-like sun-block, or risking a pimple. God forbid a pimple! Pimples are very much to be avoided in Italy. Forget going short-sighted, Italians say that *acne* is the inevitable result of indulging in prolonged sessions of frenzied masturbation. Whilst this is used by parents to discourage self-gratificatory behaviour, it also means that unfortunate teenagers with zits are not only called "pizza face", but also… well., something rather more embarrassing. It's easy to see why Sicilians choose to tan, and to hell with the crows' feet.

This leads me onto one of the major problems I have in Sicily – estimating people's age.

Correctly guessing age is important in Sicily. In many situations, choosing the right word for "you" depends on whether the person you are addressing is older or younger than you. Beyond this, Italian culture in general is very age-conscious. They have a deeply-entrenched gerarchy going on here. The young have to defer to the superior knowledge of the old in nearly all situations.

Estimating the age of an English person is fairly straightforward. It depends merely on assessing the degree of facial wrinkle perfusion and then cross-referencing this to the frumpiness of their clothes as a double-check.

In Sicily the procedure is infinitely more complex. There are so many more input-factors that the necessary calculation relies on a lengthy algorithm. The first problem is that the wrinkliness-to-age correlation is not linear. People who spend large amounts of their time sunbathing or engaged in outdoor work – which as we know covers most of population of Sicily - develop a wrinkle-quotient that far exceeds that which an English person could ever achieve over a normal lifespan.

Thus, to make the initial calculation, it is necessary to assess the quantity of crevices per facial square centimetre, and then divide this wrinkle-quotient by the depth of skin tone, a measurement which, again, has to be adjusted by the ethnic multiplier.

For example, a person with Moorish ancestry, featuring black hair and eyes, will naturally start off with far darker skin than someone descended mainly from Sicily's Greek or Spanish occupiers, who will in turn be darker than a genetic heir of the Norman invaders with green eyes and light brown hair, and so on. (Sicilians take great interest in skin tone. Whenever a baby is born everyone crowds around and discusses what type of *carnagione*, or skin tone, they think the baby has. Dark like Daddy? Pale like Mummy? Super-dark like Granny Pina? They hardly have time to get onto whose nose the baby has got.)

Once you have calculated the wrinkle-quotient-to-ethnically-weighted-skin-tone-ratio, this needs to be cross referenced to dress sense. Here again, Sicilians cheat. Women as old as sixty, with a nine-month-gestation size paunch, will happily wear skin-tight luminous yellow lycra vest tops and shorts, proudly displaying their deeply tanned cellulite-lined midriff criss-crossed with stretch marks; or perhaps a transparent black lace blouse and a pair of shiny red leggings replete with visible labels, and silver and diamante stilettoes to accessorise. Clearly this renders the clothing cross-reference factor unreliable or, at best, very tricky to estimate.

The boats again - this area is usually thronging
with fishermen selling fish and seafood, VERY fresh

The upshot of all this is that nearly all Sicilians think I am barely out of my teens and talk to me very patronisingly as a consequence. They assume a didactic attitude while they tell me obvious things. Meanwhile I tend to assume they are all about the age of my mother, and therefore anticipate forgetfulness and the inability to throw away junk mail without reading it first. Then, when I have had enough time to stare at their faces and carry out highly complex mental arithmetic, I conclude that.... they are about my age! Eventually, in many cases, it has eventually cropped up in conversation that they are actually *younger* than me. Ahem! When that happens, I am never quite sure who is more embarrassed.

So, as spring blossoms, I have decided that the rule of my life must be, balance in all things. I don't want to hasten the development of wrinkles, but I don't want rickets either. So I am going in the sun. But not for too long. I'll put on a bit of sunscreen, but not too much. And God forbid I should develop a single pimple!

One-man donkey transport: the perfect replacement for the motorbike?

With the price of petrol in Italy rising over *Euro* 1.80 a litre, and political protest-strikes blockading supplies and creating shortages... perhaps Sicilians should revert to their traditional mode of transport?

These beautiful horse (and sometimes donkey) drawn carts, called *Carretti Siciliani*, were used to transport people and goods up to the nineteen fifties. My husband remembers plenty of men were still selling fruit and veg off the back of them in the 1970's.

Nowadays they are maintained by enthusiasts, and mainly used in processions and village festivals. I took these photos at the Bagheria festival last summer.

The people riding on the carts are wearing Sicilian national costume. Many of them, mainly the older men, were singing Sicilian folk songs. They accompanied themselves with tambourines and piano accordions. To the untrained ear they sound slightly reminiscent of Arabic music, making the same use of quarter-tones and minor keys.

Ideal family transport? Save money, save the environment.

Not a very comfortable ride - there is no suspension, no rubber on the wheels, and the seat is often just seven inches from front to back

The Palermo-style carts have a yellow background and historical battle scenes, often depicting the wars with Charlemagne

Some of the typical paintings used to decorate both horse and cart are scenes from the wars of Charlemagne

Tradition has it that the feather plumes were a decorative element added by the Spanish when they occupied Sicily

An unusual example, entirely decorated with carving instead of paint

The decoration here is of two soldiers' heads

Yellow and red, the colours of the Sicilian flag,
dominate the decoration of both horse and cart

Of course donkeys need hats. It gets very hot in the summer

How many children can you squeeze into one Sicilian carriage?

Shhhh! Let's talk about The Mafia

Calogero Vizzini, one-time Mafia boss

It is a fact universally acknowledged that any Sicilian in possession of great heaps of money is in the Mafia.

I knew I would have to broach this subject sooner or later, so I've decided to just get it over with.

The first thing you need to know, should you ever visit Sicily, is that you must NEVER EVER say the word *Mafia* out loud in public. It's strictly taboo. Sicilians adhere to the old religious belief that you must never pronounce the name of the Devil aloud, as this may summon him and unleash evil forces; and they seem to apply the same rule to the Mafia.

When Sicilians go abroad, it seems that everyone makes Mafia jokes around them, or even asks them straight to their faces if they are in the Mafia. Sicilians don't think this is funny.

Just think about it. The Mafia are serial killers. They are the reason Sicily is so poor that there are better hospitals in some African countries. Many towns in Sicily have running water no more than twice a week. The streets have potholes big enough to hide a Fiat Punto. Rubbish piles up mountain high in the streets. The town halls and schools have masonry falling off them and holes in the roofs. And the authorities do nothing about any of this, because they have no money, apparently: the taxes everyone pays are all being "eaten", as Sicilians say... in other words, pocketed by the Mafia.

Shortly after I moved to Sicily I asked my husband the worst thing he had ever seen done by the Mafia. He comes from a rough area of Palermo called Brancaccio, famous for being the place where the Mafia assassinated the local priest. My husband pointed out the bullet holes in the shop facades along the local high street, the remains of shoot-outs that took place in the 1970's. He mentioned that most people in the neighbourhood respected a self-imposed curfew when he was a boy, staying inside and lowering the metal shutters

56

covering their windows after 6pm to avoid the risk of catching stray bullets. And he did reveal that he had once had to step over a dead body lying in the road on his way to school one morning.

Probably the single most damaging thing the Mafia does to Sicily nowadays is to cripple businesses.

Salvatore Giuliano assassinated by the Mafia

To run a business in Sicily takes a lot of nerve. When a start-up business has to pay legitimate taxes to the state, and then pay the same amount or more to the Mafia, where are the funds to re-invest and develop the business? The only companies that succeed seem to be the ones run by Mafia members, or family associates of the Mafia. I know too many people who had to close up shop, because they were being charged so much by the Mafia that they could not make ends meet.

You need a lot of certificates of authorisation for this, that and the other to run a business in Sicily. One of them is the Anti-Mafia Certificate issued by the police, which proves you are 'clean.' To get this certificate your whole family is checked for Mafia connections. If anyone, including first or second cousins, uncles and grandparents, is known to have had any involvement with the Mafia, you will not get this certificate.

It is a crime to pay *pizzo* - extortion money - to the Mafia nowadays, without reporting it to the police as soon as the gun or cudgel has been removed from the vicinity of your head. If you do report it, you have to hope no corrupt policeman, who has seen your official report, reveals to the Mafia that you have obeyed the law; as this will result in getting your shop and maybe your home firebombed. If you choose not to report it to anyone, you risk being imprisoned for supporting the Mafia when the Inland Revenue asks where those sums of money went.

The businessman's third option, for the most daring, or maybe the most angry, is to join the 'Addiopizzo' movement. These people openly display a sticker on the door of their premises which indicates that they are against paying extortion money and are cooperating with the police in identifying Mafiosi who come asking for it. They are courageous and lead very stressful lives. Many of them die young.

The Italian witness protection programme is nothing like the US witness protection programme portrayed in Hollywood films. Round here, you're on your own. Our local electrical goods shop was firebombed because they refused to pay the pizzo when it was asked for three times in a row. The owners lived in a flat above the shop and both livelihood and home were destroyed in one night. The four-storey cement building was almost completely razed to the ground and the couple's children were hospitalised. So were several families who lived in other flats in the block, who had nothing to do with the shop owners. Several small children and a baby ended up in a critical condition in intensive care because of smoke damage to their lungs. The police turned up when the fire brigade had finished dousing the building and the ashes were smouldering over in the early hours of the morning.

Arsenal confiscated by the police

Most Sicilians never make a stand against the Mafia because they are too scared. They live permanently in one of those situations we all know, where everyone is thinking the same thing, but nobody wants to be the one who opens their mouth and says it.

And the other reason the people here rarely talk about the Mafia openly is that, frankly, we are so fed up with it we just cannot bear to talk about it any more.

Finally, if you want to know more about the Sicilian Mafia, here's a word of warning. I have read more garbage written about this topic than I have on any other subject, ever. Anyone who claims to have the "inside story" is simply lying; if they did know anything secret, they would immediately get assassinated for writing it.

Burger King's latest offering,
available worldwide

Word is going round that Burger King has decided to "invest in Palermo". They are opening several new restaurants including a giant drive-through (or should I say drive-thru?). Not to be outdone, McDonalds has stepped up its game and is also raising its profile in the Palermo area. Both Hubby and The Godmother are disgusted.

My initial reaction was to scoff at the idea that any Italians, especially my beloved lazy Sicilians, would ever abandon their tradition of daily four-hour pasta-guzzling sessions in favour of lunching on a sandwich wrapped in polystyrene.

Yet, it turns out, they are. The Americans have clearly realised that Sicilians have a special affinity for fried food, and that good money can be made out of it.

The reason this bothers me is not that I am concerned for Sicilians' arteries. I am far too late for that. It is just very sad that the monotonous uniformity the United States has already inflicted on itself is spreading relentlessly to the rest of the world.

Sicilians simply don't need foreign fast food. Many classic Sicilian foods are fast food anyway. The Sicilians invented fast food centuries before a mad Armenian genius named Roland McDoughnut™ realised he could become a billionaire if he tipped his entire chemistry set into a sizzling chip pan, dressed up as a clown, and sold the resulting cuisine to everyone cursed with an appetite so powerful they could not wait more than four minutes for a cholesterol sandwich with a side order of deep-fried diabetes.

In fact, the Sicilians were the very first people in the world to realise that fat is delicious. When it comes to serving saturated fat and refined sugar in concentrations denser than a black hole, no nation on earth can rival their flair and imagination.

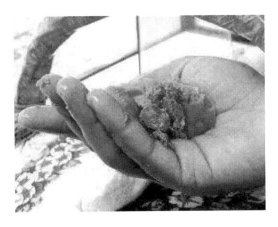

Frittola, available in Palermo only

I am not unwilling to give credit where credit is due. I take my hat off to the Scots for inventing the deep-fried, battered Mars Bar. I award an honourable mention to the Navaho tribe of America whose 'Navaho fry-bread' soaks up so much oil it can even turn a farmer's pick-up truck see-through if you swipe it along the side. I acknowledge that Yorkshire lardy cake, that sugared delicacy with a solid plug of lard at the centre, is a merit-worthy effort. Yet the gold medal, without dispute, goes to the citizens of Palermo for inventing the 'frittola'.

A **frittola** is made from a hand-picked blend of chunks of animal fat from which any trace of meat has been carefully trimmed away. These flavoursome morsels are deep fried in sizzling oil until they turn golden and crispy, and then stored inside a closed basket, ready for customers. Once a hungry punter turns up at the counter, a Sicilian "Chef" pokes his hairy hand through a hole in the basket and extracts a fistful of this filling, which he crams to overflowing into a bread roll steeped in lashings of melted lard. Eating one of these made a friend of my husband's gain three stone in a single evening and, by the time he got home, he was so tightly wedged behind the steering wheel that the only way his wife could get him out of the car was to buy another frittola and use it to lubricate his belly and breasts.

This particular delicacy is not really to my taste, I must admit, but there are alternatives to suit every palate. '**U pane cu meusa**,' for example, is a subtle blend of stir-friend spleen, parmesan cheese and lemon juice, served in a bun.

Palermo's most highly esteemed **spleen sandwich** chef is known as Nino Ballerino, or Nino The Dancer, for the elegance with which he assembles lunch for several hundred customers a day on a pavement outside his café, near the Supreme Court of Palermo. Health-conscious enforcers of justice flock to his café in their lunch hours because of his unique knack of wringing about half a pint of surplus oil out of the spleen before tossing it into the bread roll.

When my husband took me there for a quick snack dinner, I timed Nino assembling five of these in twenty five seconds. He can hold three bread rolls in one hand at a time and flip spleen into all three at once with the other. He did a five-year apprenticeship in a chippie in South End before gaining his PhD in Cholesterology, and can speak fairly fluent cockney when pressed.

Another Palermo classic is the **stigghiola**, a flame-grilled small-intestine kebab. A sheep's ileum is wound tightly around the whole length of a spring onion and grilled on a street corner by the Stigghiolaro, a Sicilian word I can only translate as 'Small intestine kebab chef'.

A stigghiolaro may seem to have a humble profession, but they are esteemed as folk heroes for their ability to spend twelve-hour working shifts inhaling smoke so thick and pungent it would make mere mortals need artificial resuscitation and maybe an oxygen mask. They tolerate a constant dousing by droplets of hot fat and, not least, they stay alive despite dining on small intestines for lunch and dinner almost every day of their lives.

One of my husband's old school friends was a stigghiolaro. He was a cheerful and spherical fellow who lived inside an impenetrable column of smoke which rendered him invisible and rose to the stratosphere where it spread out into an atomic mushroom shape, visible across the whole bay of Palermo and, on a good day, as far away as Sardinia. His petite and beautiful wife had to wash all his clothes three times to get the greasy smell out of them when he got home from work.

One day the council revoked his license because they thought his stall was lowering the tone of the neighbourhood and, unable to find a new pitch elsewhere, he had to take a job in a supermarket. The locals still lament the disappearance of Signor Gianfortuna the Stigghiolaro, but his wife's laundry burden has plummeted and so has his weight. The first time I saw him after he changed jobs I almost walked straight past him. He had changed into a slim young man with a neck.

Will the rest of these folk heroes and colourful characters gradually fade away as naive young Sicilians, attracted by the novelty and foreignness of it all, start hanging out at Burger King and McDonalds instead? I fear that they will. By the time Sicilians realise what they have lost, it will be too late.

Worse, I fear that the Sicilians will lose their tradition of sit-down family meals, and pick up the bad habits that Americans invented and Northern Europeans have already copied, forgetting that mealtimes are not just about eating, but about bonding and communicating as a family. How many of our social ills can be attributed to the disintegration of the nuclear family? And how much of this can be blamed on the fact that we sometimes go for entire days without all sitting down together, and actually paying attention to each other?

A De Luxe Day in Luxurious Sciacca

Well, we've got so much to catch up on. I think, this time, I'll tell you about the lovely sunny day we had at Sciacca with my sister-in-law and her family.

My brother-in-law is the manager of a Rocco Forte hotel - oops no, I mean luxury spa and resort - which sports two exclusive golf courses, six elite de luxe tennis courts, a luxury Olympic size swimming pool and, if you need even more space than that, three kilometres of luxurious private beach (with imported de luxe sand), a Michelin starred chef in each of its various luxury restaurants and of course, for your convenience, a luxury helicopter landing pad by which you may arrive, in luxury.

Luxury Luxury Luxury.

The name of this ineffably luxurious hotel is "Vegetable". Yeah, OK, it's in Italian which is Verdura, but that's what it means, Vegetable.

I wonder if they had a competition among the staff, and let the chef choose this name. Perhaps if the helicopter landing pad supervisor had won, he would have named the place Skids. Or maybe the pool keeper would have liked it to be called Chlorine. The laundry room supervisor dearly hoped it would be named Starch whilst the chamber maids formed a consortium to campaign for the name Tip.

Whatever.

A sea view from the town of Sciacca

We reaped the benefit, because my brother in law has been picking up tips from the chef. And not only on how to cook vegetables! He and my sis-in-law prepared us a banquet. There was risotto with cuttlefish ink sauce and flaked almonds, there were char-grilled courgettes and peppers, barbecued chicken and sausages, octopus and potato salad with garlic and parsley dressing... oh I cannot even mention any more as I feel too full already.

It was LUXURIOUS.

After that we played with my cute little nephew, and then decided to take a walk around Sciacca. The town is set on a hill over the coast and therefore has endless opportunities to take in spectacular views out across the open sea. The shops are full of tempting wares, dazzlingly coloured Sicilian ceramics and stylish Italian clothes. And ice cream parlours. Once you have gone beyond the point of no return, there is really no point in fretting over just a few extra thousand calories in a massive ice cream sundae, is there?

So there you have it, a brief outline of my luxurious day out.

A Terrible Boob

After returning from our exciting summer trip to England, I have to admit this summer has dragged somewhat. To break up the monotony of my little boy's three-month school holidays, I used ice cream.

Do you think I'm a bad mother?

We've been to the beach and got sunburn, we've collected every size and shape of pebble ever washed up by a high tide, we've glued shells on boxes, we've made origami peacocks and constructed a solar system on the kitchen table using toast and mugs and the salt cellar, we've vegetated in front of the TV (Aaaaghghhh! Yes!!!) and now, dammit, we're going out for some ice cream. Again.

Sometimes when we are out and about, we bump into the postman, and he pulls up on his bicycle and hands me a letter or two. Sometimes he delivers us a package containing toys sent from my family in England. My son is convinced they are gifts from the postman, and so he tends to greet the fellow with more enthusiasm than he usually demonstrates to his own father.

He is amazingly energetic for a man close to retirement age. One day I spotted him walking along the sea front, eating an ice cream with another, older man, whom he introduced as the previous postman. The Ex-postman had lived in America for eight years.

"Howdy" he greeted me, with a strong Italian accent. "'Ow y'all doin'a?"

"Oh, fine, thank you," I said, trying not to laugh. He was very proud of his knowledge of English. I could tell it added to his status in the village.

"Y'all 'avin' yourself ha mighty nice day now," he said, tipping his peaked cap as he walked on, and carefully poking his little scoop back into his ice cream.

A couple of weeks later I spotted this ex postman with another man, even older than himself. This old fellow was wrinklier than a raisin, but he still walked at a lively pace.

"Howdy folks!" I called out. I am not certain why I said this, but it seemed the appropriate thing to say, at the time.

"Howdy!" responded the ex-postman.

He then introduced me to his companion, who was *his* predecessor, the ex-ex postman. This charming fellow said he was ninety-seven years old and was the oldest person in the village.

"So your predecessor isn't still around, then?" I asked the ex-ex-postman in Italian.

"No, there wasn't a post office in the village before me," he answered.

Just then the village idiot pedalled past at a leisurely pace on his bicycle.

"Hello Giuseppe" they both called out, and looked relieved when he cycled past ignoring them.

The village idiot always rides his bicycle around, in no particular direction, and people fly out of his way, dropping babies, or bags of vegetables, or whatever they are holding, with reckless abandon in their haste to clear a path for him. This is because he has customised his bicycle in such a way that he cannot see where he is going.

He has painted it fuchsia pink and twined ribbons gaily around the entire frame, he has embellished the wheels with fluttering ribbons and, most importantly, he has somehow attached a music stand to the handlebars, rising up well above his line of vision and displaying photographs of all his favourite football players, taped on firmly.

He occasionally hits unmovable objects such as parked cars, and simply gets back on his bicycle, apparently unperturbed, and continues on his way. On this particular occasion he scored a direct hit against a lamppost and he and his bicycle flew off in opposite directions. As he picked up his bike he apologised to the lamppost, realigned his music stand and continued on his way.

After watching him roll off down the road, the ex-postman and the ex-ex-postman said they were on their way to the ice-cream parlour, and invited me to join them. My friend Giuseppe was there, keenly awaiting company, as the ice-cream vending business was always slack at this time of day and things could get lonely. Giuseppe of the ice cream parlour is not to be confused with Giuseppe the Village Idiot, Giuseppe the butcher, or any of the other Giuseppes in the village. It's quite handy that three-quarters of the males in the village are called Giuseppe, as it is easier to remember everyone's name.

I ordered a coffee granita and an ice-cream sandwich. A granita is basically a 'slush puppie' and, if it is a coffee one, that means a cold double espresso has been tipped in with the ice. It was delicious, but I had failed to take into consideration that I am unaccustomed to such quantities of caffeine, and consequently developed a severe, Parkinson's-type hand tremor which made eating my ice-cream sandwich a hazardous challenge to my grossly impaired eye-hand coordination.

My ice cream brioche...
they could have filled it a bit more!

The ice-cream sandwich is a Sicilian speciality which consists of the largest possible quantity of ice-cream wedged firmly into a hamburger-style bread roll. The bread is soft and slightly sweet with a hint of vanilla. The whole thing is ambrosial, provided you are capable of eating it without shaking uncontrollably and thus launching the ice cream component of it down your own cleavage at high velocity, then quickly grabbing it back and ramming the entire thing into your mouth in one go, hoping the ex-postman and the ex-ex-postman have not noticed what you are doing and, as a consequence, developing the worst ice-cream brain-freeze you have ever suffered in your life, so severe that your ears almost fall off and you cannot speak because your tongue is cryogenically frozen onto your soft palate.

Unfortunately Giuseppe of the ice-cream parlour did notice what I was doing. Now who was the idiot of the village?

I think Giuseppe enjoyed the part where I furtively fondled my own breasts, because since then he has been offering me free ice-cream every time I go in there.

I have not concerned myself too much with his motives. Acts of generosity should always be accepted graciously, shouldn't they? I can certainly be gracious. I have become a regular, almost daily, customer of his, actually.

On balance, it hasn't been such a bad summer after all. And my son thinks I am a *wonderful* mother.

Manna from Heaven? Or from Sicily?

This summer we went for a day trip to a town called Castelbuono.

If you speak Italian you'll know that this means "good castle". The place is well named because there *is* a castle there, and it *is* pretty good actually. It's medieval, huge, has a scary portcullis and a massive dungeon, a secret underground tunnel leading you to the church, and there are countless places with no handrail where an inattentive six-year-old (or a woman who doesn't know how to negotiate cobblestones in high heels) could fall about 30 feet onto a solid slab of rock.

Castelbuono castle, where handrails are notable for their absence

To be brutally honest, it's not quite as good as the castle at Caccamo. In *that* Medieval castle, there is a carved wooden altar opposite the long dining table, with an antique rug upon which visitors could kneel while praying. But – aha! - the rug hides a trap door, operated by a lever the other side of the room. The wicked count who owned this castle would lure his enemies into his home with the offer of lavish dinners, feigned friendship and terribly expensive imported wines; wait till they were inspired by the urge to pray (they *were* Medieval, after all); and then send them down the chute directly into his dungeon, which had no exit. Then he would sit back down, thump his fist on the dining table and shout "More capons and a flagon of wine, wench!" as he listened to his victim howling about having two broken legs, probably.

Caccamo castle...watch where you tread!

As I said, Castelbuono's castle is not quite as exciting as that one, but it's well worth a visit. The chapel is particularly astonishing, with several hundred sculpted cherubs appearing to emerge out of the walls rather like ghosts.

The town of Castelbuono is also a wonderful place to spend a day. It has bars on every corner which sell mouth-watering sorbet ice cream, home-made from fruits such as mandarins and mulberries and watermelons. It has a cavernous and jaw-dropping antique shop (it's not just the prices that are jaw-dropping, the antiques are spectacular too). It also has a very exciting emporium where they bring in organic meat from surrounding farms and make exotic sausages and salami and other meat dishes. Castelbuono is one of the centres of the "Slow Food Association", an organization which encourages the appreciation of top quality food, eaten with the respect and enjoyment it deserves.

Yet even this isn't what makes Castelbuono really exciting. In Castelbuono, you can eat Manna.

Yes Manna, that stuff in the bible, which falls out of the sky.

"And when the dew that lay was gone up, behold, upon the face of the wilderness there lay a small round thing, as small as the hoar frost on the ground. And when the children of Israel saw it, they said one to another, It is manna: for they wist not what it was. And Moses said unto them, This is the bread which the Lord hath given you to eat. This is the thing which the Lord hath commanded, Gather of it every man according to his eating."

Exodus 16:14-16

Manna falling from a tree... rather than from heaven

Manna is the sap of the manna tree, a type of narrow-leaf ash called *fraxinus angustifolia*. The manna trees have grown wild around Castelbuono for many centuries. They grow in the Central and Western Mediterranean, and so may be indigenous to Sicily. Since they recently began to become rare in the mountains around Castelbuono, they are now cultivated as well.

In July and August, the creamy white sap flows so abundantly that it drips out of the branches and gradually crystallises, so it looks like icicles hanging off the tree. Local experts - generally, very small, very old men who look a lot like Getafix The Druid - know how to cut slits in the bark to create far more of these stalactites than occur naturally, and they monitor the trees over many days as they extend ever downwards. They are cut from the tree when they reach the ground.

Manna only contains about 3% glucose, which makes it very useful for diabetics. In Sicily, if you flick a cupcake into a crowd, it has a 99.9% probability of landing on someone diabetic.

It is about 45% mannitol, a type of sugar that is absorbed very slowly and which has laxative effects if you eat too much of it. Being constipated is the Italian national sport (serves them right for eating pasta all the time), so this is touted as its other great medicinal property. It is also another bonus for diabetics, of course: nobody will scoff all the manna when they're not looking. If anyone does, Diabetic Uncle Danilo will stake out the loo and expose the culprit!

A number of ludicrously extravagant claims have been made for the magical medicinal properties of Manna. I was told by various vendors in Castelbuono that it will cure all allergies. It will cure any liver disease. It will even cure death – honestly, one woman said that. It does contain various useful nutrients such as zinc, but frankly, the main reason for eating it is just that it tastes really nice.

If you go to Castelbuno, you can eat manna ice cream, too. Just don't have too much! Uncle Danilo may be watching!

The Villa Romana Del Casale, Piazza Armerina

This post is about a UNESCO world heritage site in Sicily! Classy or what?

There are altogether 44 UNESCO world heritage sites in Italy. The criteria are that World Heritage Sites can be "natural" or "cultural" places of general wonderfulness. That's my handy summary of a long and tedious paragraph. Interestingly enough, the UK only has 28 of them, and the USA has an embarrassingly modest 21. I bet they wish they'd been invaded by the Romans! Meanwhile Germany has a hefty score of 37. Now I'm beginning to smell a rat. How can they possibly have that many? I've been to Germany, all over the place. They have lovely sausages and it's very clean but, come off it! World heritage sites? I like Germans a lot but, let's face it, Germany's boring. I mean, *really* boring. I've just checked and found that Greece has a mere seventeen sites of outstandingly superlative phenomenalness (or whatever it was). Now I know that this whole system is fiddled and meaningless.

And let's come back to the USA. Much as it pains me to pass up any opportunity to take the mickey out of Yanks – it's one of my more constructive hobbies - I have to admit that the American countryside is breath-taking, staggering, full of uniqueness and generally, everywhere you go, utterly marvellous. If they've only registered 21 sites so far, it's bound to be because they're too busy hiking around all the rest and enjoying the views. Canada also has just 16. I've never been to Canada but I'd love to go, and I bet they have far more stunning places than 16.

The Roman Villa del Casale in South-Eastern Sicily villa was built in the 4th century AD and was used continuously until it was buried by a landslide in the 12th century. The villa was huge and would have been built and decorated at staggering expense. It was the manor house of a colossal agricultural estate, owned and run by an Italian aristocrat. Sicily was regarded as a terribly primitive province by the Romans (it still is) but farms here were prized, as the land was so fertile.

Anyway, what do you think of the place?

72

Do you iron your socks?

Sicilian housewives do. They iron all their towels and underpants as well, apparently.

My mother-in-law, aka The Godmother, dropped in yesterday afternoon. Despite our tense relationship, we have found an uneasy truce, based on the fact that she finds ironing so relaxing she is willing to do mine when she has run out of her own.

My own idea of relaxing is to eat chocolates and drink red wine while watching TV, but The Godmother doesn't let me relax while she is busy relaxing. She assigns me tasks.

Yesterday, she decided to teach me how to iron properly for myself. Using her iron.

My Iron

The Godmother's iron

First she made me gather up the dry laundry. I pottered about sorting it into two heaps; one Mount Everest of things that needed ironing; and a Mount Etna that I could fold and put away.

The Godmother popped over to check, and pointed out that I had committed another of my gross domestic blunders. Everything needs ironing!

"What, even towels?" I dared to ask.

The Godmother thought I was just saying this to make her laugh.

She rolled up her sleeves.

"I'll show you the best way to iron," she offered enthusiastically. "I have a personal ironing technique which can flatten anything." She picked up all the clothes and reunited them into a single heap.

I wondered whether to tell her that in England we avoid ironing our jeans because the few people who walk round with a crease down the front of a pair of Levi's are simply marking themselves out as illegal immigrants, indeed, that in England we think people who iron their jeans or T-shirts are sick and wrong, and must be stopped. I also wondered what she would think if I told her there was no need to iron her son's pants because he pressed them nice and flat himself with the warmth of his own buttocks as soon as he put them on. If I were a braver person I might also have mentioned that I preferred his pyjamas nice and wrinkly and, really, I was the only person he was supposed to impress when dressed in them.

In the end, I was afraid to tell her, so I remained silent.

When I was a financial analyst, I calmly met the directors of listed companies which had revenues of millions of pounds a day, and I was not afraid to tell them they were making mistakes in the way they ran their companies and should change a lot of things. If I believed a man was not handling his assets to their best advantage, I set him straight. If I thought someone's gross margin was pathetic, I said so.

Now, as an apprentice Sicilian housewife, I was standing opposite The Godmother and she was telling me to iron her son's underpants, and I was too scared to say no. I obeyed.

The Godmother should not really be frightening as a person. She is about a foot shorter than me (albeit two feet wider) and she is old and wrinkly as well. It is just that she has eyes that look as if she could make streaks of lightning come flashing out of them at will, and reduce any adversary who refuses to wash their face again, and do it properly this time, to a smoking heap of ashes. And those shovel hands of hers were simply created for spanking. I am quite sure one solid slap on the botty, from her, could actually send a fully grown male, even one who routinely eats *frittola*, into low earth orbit.

Her patented ironing technique involved heating the iron to a temperature that could smelt many types of metal ore, and then release a full litre of water vapour into the atmosphere, via the fibres of the offending wrinkly garment, with each push of the 'steam' button.

Her iron was no normal iron. It was attached to a large tank which continually refilled it with water via a flexible hose and featured a control panel allowing her to adjust the water temperature and pressure, the iron temperature, the steam squirting rate and many other variables I would only have thought relevant to a space shuttle.

Whilst she twiddled the dials and gave me a stream of enthusiastic explanations, I am ashamed to say my mind wandered. It does have an inconvenient tendency to go meandering off on its own, without its owner's permission, from time to time.

The Godmother and I define ourselves in different ways, I realised.

Don't we all have things we've done, or things we do, that we feel are the essence of our personality? I think those are the things by which we want others to judge us. For me, my degree in Classics, my career as a financial adviser, the fact I have travelled to many countries and have friends from all over the world – these are some of the things that make up the woman I want other people to see. I'm a housewife now, but it's just what I'm doing, it's not who I am. I call myself "The Sicilian Housewife" as a joke, you see. I only want to be a housewife the way Marie Antoinette wanted to be a shepherdess. I don't *actually* want to be good at it.

The Godmother defines herself as a lifetime professional housewife. If a member of her family is wearing something a bit creased, if anyone doesn't like something she's cooked for them, if there's a speck of dust on her kitchen floor, she feels like a failure as a person.

Most Sicilian women seem to be like her. They tell you how much stuff they've ironed, or describe what they made for dinner last night, by way of conversation. It took me a long time living in Sicily to realise that they're showing off.

They cannot understand why I don't want to compete. I would far rather spend an hour helping my son to practise reading than pressing his pants. I'm happy for him to have mud on his backside, so long as he's having fun. If my floor is dusty but I've spent the morning reading a volume of George Vancouver's diary describing the tribes of north Western Canada, I feel utterly fulfilled as a human being.

Well, the result of my philosophical reverie was that I nearly casseroled my hand, while it was still attached to my arm, by pressing the "eject gusts of vapour at a temperature hotter than the core of the sun" button instead of the "start super-cooling down to ambient temperature over the course of the next four days" button.

Whilst I nursed my hand with a bag of frozen peas, The Godmother attacked a ribbed jumper.

"I'll get all those nasty ridges out of this in no time" she said. She then proceeded to press my jumper so vehemently that by the time she had finished with it, it did indeed no longer have any ridges. It was no longer a ribbed jumper. It was smooth, and four feet wide.

After that she pressed the towels till they were as thin and absorbent as muslin, melted the elastic on all my knickers, and removed the cartoon characters off the front of my son's T-shirts by making them simply atomise at the temperature of a red dwarf. I was getting scared she might decide to iron me next. Seriously, I was panicking.

Luckily, she felt relaxed enough to stop at that point, and permitted me to put everything away.

Maybe I could interest her in extreme ironing next? I think that might be her ideal sport.

Extreme ironing involves carrying an ironing board to the most inaccessible places on earth, such as the top of Mount Everest, and doing some ironing there.

I wonder if The Godmother would find that relaxing.

79

The Villa of the Monsters in Bagheria

We have a very bizarre tourist attraction in our town.

Villa Palagonia has been nicknamed the Villa of the Monsters locally for centuries. It is absolutely crammed with caricature stone sculptures of bizarre creatures, deformed little men, goblins, and ugly hybrid "manimals".

On the perimeter wall; the sculpture on the left shows my next door neighbour riding her husband; on the right is a portrayal of Silvio Berlusconi planning his next election campaign

It was visited in the 18th century by multi-talented German writer, politician, lawyer and bore, Johann "Sausages" Von Goethe. When Goethe visited the villa, its owner, the inveterate trickster Ferdinando Gravina, gave him a joke chair to sit on. It was invisibly held together with fragile splints of wood. When Herr Goethe lowered his sturdy Teutonic buttocks upon its seat, he crashed to the floor amid a pile of sticks. Apparently he was not amused.

Approaching the villa, you first pass through the gateposts to the original grounds. Several streets festooned with laundry and dented cars have now been built between them and the villa itself. As you draw nearer, you keep spotting stone dogs playing violins and donkeys riding upon women with three tits, glimpsed between fluttering pairs of humungous knickers.

Eventually you reach the second pair of gates, flanked by statues of ugly, goblin-like beings about nine feet tall, tightly wedged between a ticket booth and a ladies clothing shop.

The entrance gate by the ticket booth; a few steps to the left you can stock up on all the sequinned hotpants you'll ever need

When you walk in through the gates you see the beautiful facade of the villa at the end of a broad, sandy path lined with oleanders, orange trees, cacti, and flowering trees. Don't go looking off to the right! You'll be faced with a row of private back gardens full of plastic slides, see-saws, abandoned tricycles, a few parked cars and the ubiquitous Sicilian laundry hung up to dry.

"Che schifo" said my husband the first time we saw this.

This literally means "How disgusting." Sicilians say it very often. They say it with great passion and feeling, none with more passion and feeling than my Hubby. "Che schifo," he said again. "Che vergogna. How shameful! Che schifo!"

Trying to put this behind us, we hastened around the other side of the garden and admired the view of the villa from the back – or was if the front? It seemed to have two fronts, each completely different from the other. You can easily get from one side of the villa to the other by walking under an archway that passes through the centre of the buildings. But look out! Don't get garotted by the washing line! The aristocratic heirs of this villa still live in it, and there's always a few noble panty-girdles and baronial-looking jeans with balloon seats drying under there.

There's a slideshow lower down, by the way, so if you're getting bored you can just scroll down to that, and then click off somewhere else. Don't forget to click on the "like" button before you go.

Well, construction of the villa began in 1715. Work on the villa proceeded at Sicilian speed, which is just a little slower then geological speed. Whenever you see a Sicilian man working in a hole in the road, there will be a thronging crowd of others standing around watching him and making helpful suggestions, or simply appreciating his artfulness and egging him on. Villa Palagonia was constructed in this manner. There's very little a Sicilian man enjoys more than admiring someone else working hard, during his own leisure time.

A full twenty-two years after it was started, the fifth Prince Don Ferdinand was dead and his son began work on the lower floors which surround the villa. Finally, the grandson of the founder of the villa was ready to get cracking on the interior décor in 1749.

This Seventh Prince of Palagonia was quite a nutter. He was the mastermind behind the hall of mirrors, which local legend has it was designed to torment his young wife and drive her to utterly lose her mind through fear of its spookiness. The Hall of mirrors is the main room of the very small part of the villa actually open to the public.

When the villa was built, mirrors were the most expensive items one could possibly use for interior decor, short of using solid slabs of pure gold. A method of backing a plate of flat glass with a thin sheet of tin and mercury was first developed in Venice during the 16th century. Up until this time, a mirror has simply been a very polished piece of metal.

For a long time the Venetians held a monopoly in the business of mirror production. Apparently the French lured some Venetian mirror makers away to build the legendary hall of mirrors in the Palace of Versailles. The government of the Venetian Republic was so keen to protect their monopoly that they hired professional assassins to track them down and poison them. Or it was it just those frogs' legs and snails the French kept giving them to eat?

Anyway, the decision to cover the entire ceiling of this hall in Bagheria with mirrors was a deliberate display of vulgar ostentation.

This was a time when the Sicilian Barons were filthy rich. Ships from all the seagoing European countries would stop off in the bay of Palermo and fill their holds with Sicilian oranges and lemons, to stop their smelly sailors from getting scurvy on the high seas. On their way back from trading raids in Asia they'd stop off again. By this time they'd usually been drinking their own piss for months and were so scorbutic they had seeping wounds and wobbly teeth, but their holds were crammed with gold doubloons, pieces of eight and literally thousands of sachets of curry powder, and a few spare parrots. They'd pay whatever price was asked for a tankard of freshly squeezed homemade organic lemonade. The Sicilian barons who owned the citrus orchards became fabulously wealthy. And of course they deserved it, for ensuring that sailors all over the world received a nutritionally balanced diet.

The first ever room equipped with mirrors on the ceiling?

The mirrors cover the ceiling. They are deliberately mounted at subtly varying angles, so that, as you walk around the room, you see yourself reflected dozens of times. Every little movement you make is magnified into the flickering of a crowd. The mirrors are also painted with birds, flowers and branches of red coral which looks disturbingly like blood seeping through the cracks.

The walls are faced with slabs of marble in dark, blood reds and maroons and other exotic colours, gathered from multiple sites around Italy and beyond. Somewhat above eye level, each panel bears a sculpture of an ancestor of the Gravina family. They look like life-size marble men and women trying to clamber out of the stonework, as if frozen in some scene from a horror film where people are entrapped and trying to escape from a virtual world. I found them fascinating and wonderful yet also disturbing.

My husband did not like them at all.

"Che scifo," he said, in fact. "These are creepy. What kind of lunatics would want to have a room like this in their house?"

The nutty count then proceeded to have the entire perimeter wall topped with gruesome sculptures. Some said they were cruel caricatures of his poor wife's various lovers, and any other person who had offended him. Others said he was simply a lunatic wasting extraordinary amounts of money on ugly and pointless "art". Whatever people thought, the locals started calling the place the "The Villa of the Monsters", and that name is still used today.

The count's style of interior décor made his demented residence famous throughout Europe. It was visited by anyone who could get themselves an invitation to enter the freaky place on their aristocratic grand tour of Europe.

Visitors included the early travel writer Henry Swinburne; Patrick Brydone, who was in Sicily because of his passionate interest in lava flows which later led him to realize the earth is far older than had hitherto been realised; English architect John Soane, upon whom the villa made a profound impact and who subsequently designed the Bank of England building; the Count de Borde, about whom I can find nothing interesting to say; the artist and travel writer Jean-Pierre Houël; and Alexandre Dumas, whom many people know as the author of the Three Musketeers but whom fewer people know was the grandson of a French nobleman and a Haitian slave, who once remarked to a man who insulted him about his mixed-race background: "My father was a mulatto, my grandfather was a Negro, and my great-grandfather a monkey. You see, Sir, my family starts where yours ends".

Perhaps the most illustrious of all visitors was the German multi-talented politician and sausage eater Goethe, who went on to write that "To have seen Italy without having seen Sicily is to not have seen Italy at all, for Sicily is the clue to everything". He didn't say a word about the trick chair or his jarred backside. He was classy that way.

The Arabic Cathedral of Monreale

Just outside Palermo, in the charming little town of Monreale, lies possibly the most beautiful - and certainly the most exotic - cathedral in Europe.

Monreale Cathedral was built by King William II of Sicily in 1174. The architecture is Moorish Arabic, the interior is late Byzantine, and the layout is a fusion of Catholic and Eastern Orthodox convention. This style of architecture is known, in Sicily, as Norman.

I love this cathedral not only for its serenity and exceptional beauty, but for the uniquely Sicilian cultural fusion it represents. Sicily was invaded and occupied many times, and this multicultural island hosted immigrants of many faiths. Muslims, Catholics, Orthodox Christians and Jews lived side by side peacefully. The Muslim rulers, in particular, taught genuine respect for all faiths and cultures.

The Muslims had ceased to rule Sicily over a hundred years ago, yet King William chose their style of architecture to build his great cathedral. Perhaps we have something to learn from those Sicilians of long ago?

Sicilian Builders and their Bottoms

I have a mild dispute going on with my husband. He wants to get a sun-roof constructed over the open-air roof terrace, so we can have barbecues up there without getting slow-roasted in the sun before our food does, and developing skin cancer before lunch is over.

I don't.

My reason is simple: it would mean letting Sicilian builders into the house, which would simply be too traumatic. And life threatening.

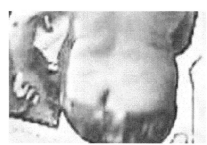

Plumber's bum, Builder's bottom, Bermondsey cleavage, Workman's Wonder.

Everyone has a traumatic builder story, I think. Nobody likes having them working in their home. But in Sicily, they are the worst in the world, I suspect.

It's not that they want a cup of tea with eight spoons of sugar in it every half hour, like English builders. It's not that they have bottoms, as in, bare ones with hairy buttock cleavages showing. It's not that they tell you they'll come on Monday morning and then show up mid-afternoon on Thursday. It's not even the fact that Sicilian builders always have to work in groups of ten, with one man doing the work while nine others watch him and egg him on by proffering constructive criticism on every move he makes.

Oh no. It's that, as we watched our house being built, it gradually became apparent that the Sicilian builders didn't know how to use spirit levels. They were ex-convicts, who had deliberately reduced their already modest intelligence quotients down to single digits by using alcohol. But they had hammers, so we couldn't challenge them.

The house looked beautiful at a casual glance but, when we moved in, it was impossible to find a right angle, a horizontal surface or, for that matter, a vertical one anywhere in the entire building. You see, if builders don't know how to use spirit levels, then buildings won't have horizontal bottoms. And if builders cannot get their bottoms right, how can their tops be OK?

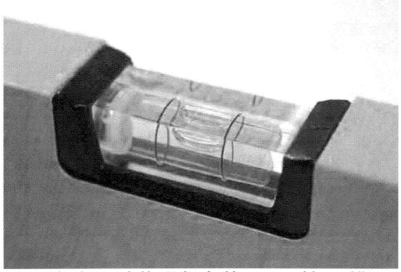

A spirit level... regarded by Sicilian builders as one of the world's great enigmas

For example:
1. The man we hired to tile the bathrooms could not find any way to disguise the fact that the shower cubicle is seven tiles wide at the bottom and eight tiles wide at the top.
2. The rectangular mirror we ordered, to be set into a space in the tiles above the sink, had to be trimmed to a rhombus to make it fit.
3. The men who fitted the overhead kitchen cupboards asked me if I wanted them to make contact with the wall "at the top", or "at the bottom." "Both" was not an option, they explained patiently.
4. The glass shelves for toiletries were aligned with the edges of the tiles. When we watched my perfume bottles go skiing one after the other onto the floor, we realised the shelf was set at a one-in-six gradient.
5. The drainage hole at the centre of the courtyard stands at the peak of a tiled summit, whilst the rainwater drains away from it into the four marshy corners, where it incubates a new generation of mosquitoes once every three hours.

Our house was built by a man called Fortunato Mastronzo. If you translate this literally into English, it means "Lucky, but a turd" – the turd part corresponding perfectly with the Italian word in both its literal and metaphorical sense.

I remember when the house was being built we arranged to meet him at the construction site. He left us waiting for two hours while the builders all sipped beer and wondered where he could have got to. Eventually he turned up with a cigarette hanging from his lip and extensive wet patches under his arms. He smelt of sweat and too much aftershave and he left us standing around for another quarter of an hour while he talked on his mobile phone, the cigarette glued to his lower lip wagging up and down dangerously until a particularly extravagant hand gesture sent it flying and he sprang backwards, brushing the scorching ash off his paunch.

We toured the developing shell of the house. When I looked at the marble windowsill in one of the bedrooms I realised it was sloping inwards, not outwards. It was angled to make all the rainwater flow straight into the room. When I pointed this out to Mr. Turd, he vigorously denied it, so I picked up an off-cut of copper piping left lying around by the plumber and placed it on the windowsill. We watched it roll rapidly towards us onto Mr. Turd's foot. He flinched when it landed and I may not have been completely sincere in my apology.

Besides never apologising for his lack of punctuality, Mr. Turd was completely unruffled by our complaints about the construction. I suppose all my frustration should have been thoroughly predictable. England's national monument is the biggest clock in the world, whereas Italy's most famous building is a tower which leans off at thirteen degrees to the perpendicular.

Big Ben... keeping Londoners
punctual for 180 years

The Leaning Tower of Pisa...
constructed entirely without the
use of spirit levels

During some of the long sleepless nights in my little crooked house, I have drawn comfort from the fact that, despite its being so squiffy, the Italian builders have nevertheless made the Leaning Tower of Pisa remain almost upright for the last eight hundred years.

Forgive me, though, if I don't want a replica of it built on top of my own house.

God Save us from Hallowe'en!

"My priest said that if I go to a Hallowe'en party I'll end up in Hell" I was told by a 10-year-old Sicilian girl yesterday.

"How can I not come to a Hallowe'en
party when it's in my own house?"

I was helping her put on her ghost costume and apply white make-up to her face, in preparation for the Hallowe'en party that her mother and I were hosting together.

"Isn't that just silly?" she asked me, asphyxiating me in a dense cloud of talcum powder. I could not breathe well enough to answer her.

Meanwhile my husband reported that a colleague of his was participating in a "Prayer Marathon" with a group from his church, to protect all good Catholics from those who invoke demons and worship the devil through their wicked Hallowe'en festivities. I could just picture the rosary beads flailing and the incense clouds billowing.

If I were living in Tibet then perhaps this level of misunderstanding might be a little more expectable. But.... Europeans? I mean, really? How is it possible there are people who don't realise Hallowe'en is no more than a great opportunity to wear funny costumes, play games and demand free sweets from strangers? Or even some finger food?

"Did you tell your colleague we're organising a Halloween party this year?" I asked my husband.

"No. He might have turned up at the house with an exorcist," answered Hubby.

Exorcists are not just from horror films in Sicily. They are actually real. Some Sicilians call them to exorcise demons from their relatives whom they believe are possessed. I once taught English to a kid whose father was an exorcist. Some of the other kids had seen him in action, and said it was very frightening. It involved candles, praying and occasional extremely loud shouting from behind a closed door. But nobody had seen any heads rotating further than would be natural, apparently.

There has been talk for a while now about Europe becoming too uniform, with all the old cultural traditions melding into one general melee of commercialised blandness. I am here to say, we are not there yet!

Have you ever had some aspect of your culture ludicrously misunderstood? Was it just funny, or really annoying?

"This is my one!"

The Black Madonna of Tindari

Yesterday we went to Tindari in Eastern Sicily, famous for its statue of a black Madonna with a black baby Jesus. It was a long drive through that beautiful Sicilian autumn sunshine, when the countryside looks lush and the higher you go, the clearer and fresher the air feels and the distances you can see seem almost impossible. It was the kind of weather that makes you realise why the ancient Romans and Greeks built temples at the tops of mountains to get closer to the gods.

The Black Madonna of Tindari
prior to recent restoration

Like most of the "black Madonna" statues from places where the majority of the population is white, she is carved out of wood, and so was originally light-skinned. Wood darkens over time so, eventually, she became black. This transformation meant she was not just another Madonna statue but, rather, something rare, precious and the product of a miracle; and so pilgrims visited her from far and wide. Among them, in 1995, was Pope John Paul II.

The Black Madonna's new church, completed in 1979

She dates from around 800 AD, according to a guide book I sneakily read beside a souvenir stand without actually buying it. We're on an economy drive at the moment, as my husband reminds me every time I go within 50 feet of any establishment that sells anything whatsoever. It took me a while to figure out why he always offers to hold my handbag when I go to the toilet. He's worried I'll get distracted on the way.

She is carved from a rare type of cedar wood which comes from Turkey and the Middle East, according to the guide book I don't have, and was brought to Sicily by sailors in the Byzantine era. Legend has it that the ship upon which she was being transported – where to, nobody knows - was driven into the bay of Tindari by a ferocious storm. The sailors dumped most of the cargo on the beach to make the ship more manoeuvrable, and set out again. Another storm blew up, more violent than the previous one, and drove them back onto the beach once more. They deposited the statue as well, the last thing they had on board, and set sail with their fingers crossed. This time they got away safely and floated off into the sunset.

Meanwhile the small number of Sicilian bumpkins who eked out a living in the remains of the once grand city of Tyndaris, founded by the Ancient Greeks, were most excited by what they found on their gorgeous strip of beach. She was already a centuries old antique, from a far off land, and she was black skinned with a black baby; yet she was clearly the Madonna with baby Jesus.

The locals took her up to their tiny church on the top of the peak overlooking the bay of Tindari, and there they prayed to her. News spread of the miraculous way she had come to Tindari, and of her remarkable black skin, and pilgrims began arriving from distant places.

The Mediterranean was plagued by pirates in those days, and a gang of Algerian desperadoes under the command of a ruthless leader called Rais Dragut (or Turgut Reis) destroyed the original church in 1544, so a new one was built as soon as possible.

This bit of history made sense of a strange tourist souvenir on sale on the walk up to the sanctuary – a collection of pirates' heads carved out of coconut shells, complete with bandanas and earrings. They were nestled among a forest of black plastic madonnas in various sizes, ranging from the 2 Euro pocket size all the way up to 30 Euro whoppers, beside mountains of rosary beads, and just in front of various black Madonna bumper stickers saying "My driver went all the way to the sanctuary of Tindari and all he bought me was this Black Madonna bumper sticker," or something along those lines: I couldn't read them properly as my husband was nervously pulling me away.

Turgut Reis: He doesn't look
much like a coconut, if I'm honest

Our Lady of Tindari now stands in a completely modern church, finished in 1979. It is decorated with mosaics and stained glass windows in fairly traditional style, yet the modern touches are obvious in all the details and, to me, this gives it rather a Disneyland feel. It is beautiful nevertheless, particularly the exterior.

The Madonna statue is displayed up on high above the altar, and beneath her is a Bible quotation in Latin, from the Song of Songs: "Nigra sum sed Formosa" – I am black but I am beautiful. I found a very interesting analysis of this book of the bible in a blog by a Brazilian priest and biblical scholar.

The interior walls of the church are entirely decorated with very fine mosaics depicting scenes from the life of the Madonna

Joseph with Jesus as a young boy. Statues and images of Joseph with the young Jesus are so common in Sicily that I think you see them more often than images of the Madonna and child. In a culture where fathers are so involved with their children and such active parents, it was inevitable that a church dedicated to the Madonna had to have at least one image of the father and son. The inscription above the statue says "Saint Joseph intervenes to help us"

This cute little carving of the last supper forms the base of the altar. It is made of marble and the figures are about the size of Barbie dolls.

The sanctuary viewed from down the hill

From the piazza in front of the church you can see marvellous views over the bay. When the sea level is low, the beach forms a strange shape which looks like the black Madonna and her child viewed side-on. Story has it that a pilgrim in early Medieval times, who had a small baby, refused to pray to the Madonna because she was black. When she left the church she slipped and dropped her baby, who slid right down to the beach but was saved from drowning by the strange strip of sand which rose up to save him, and the miracle restored her faith so she went back to the church to pray to the Madonna in thanks.

The sea was a little too high to see the profile of the Madonna properly

As we left the sanctuary I think my husband gave up a silent prayer of thanks that we had gone all round the sanctuary and the only money I spent was three euros on a little black Madonna as a gift for my mother in law, aka The Godmother.

Just 3 Euros!

Photographic talent? ...Or maybe not?

In my previous post, I described our weekend visit to Tindari to see the Black Madonna. In compliance with my husband's Great Economy Drive, a restaurant lunch was forbidden, so we had a picnic here:

"**This is so romantic!**" declared my son, who is 6 years old.

He took that photo of the sea (above), and then he took a photo of my husband and me:

Then my husband took a photo of me with our son:

I know as a wife and mother I am supposed to be encouraging to all members of the family, but when there is such a blatant discrepancy in talent, you have to face up to it. At this point, I confiscated the camera and gave it back to my son, who took these photos:

He was very interested in the various textures of the leaves and the patterns his shoes made in the sand, as well as the strong contrast between light and shade produced by the intense sunlight.

Finally, I took a picture of the little photographer:

So, who do you think has the most talent in the family?

Have we got too many immigrants?

Immigration is a hot topic in most developed countries. Apparently the Latino element in the USA turned out to vote for Barack Obama in record numbers and are now asking for immigration policy reforms, to legitimise their not-so-legal relatives as formally recognised US residents.

Olé!

These people are mainly economic migrants, though. In Sicily, we get Africans fleeing for their lives. Sicily is exactly half way between Europe and Africa, so we are in the front line.

African refugees in Lampedusa, Sicily, in a detention centre

I went through the immigration process in Italy myself when I moved here eight years ago. I tried, in those early, naïve days, to point out to anyone who would listen that there is such a thing as the European Union and that I should have the automatic right to live in Italy just because I wanted to.

That's how it works for EU citizens entering the UK.

In return a uniformed, armed policeman at the immigration office informed me that being a European citizen merely gave me the automatic right to queue hop. He withdrew his weapon, and forced me to barge straight to the front of a long line of despondent and disappointed Africans, east Europeans and assorted Asians who looked as if they had already been waiting in this dismal immigration office, lined with peeling grey paint and posters of people being deported, for about five years. I was eaten up with guilt when I saw the sadness on their faces as they realised they would have to wait even longer, probably only to receive further disappointment anyway.

"Are you sure England's in the European Union?" the policeman suddenly asked me after elbowing a Moroccan out of the way and physically manhandling me into the service booth in his place.

"Definitely," I said. "We joined before Italy, actually."

"But you don't have the Euro," he objected.

"And a good thing too, don't you think?" I answered.

The policeman liked my comment so much he leaned into the booth and told the official to make sure my case was passed without any setbacks or faffing around.

"And don't overdo the stapling either," he added. "She's English, so don't waste her time."

Italian officials love to string things out, so they not only keep foreign people waiting for inordinate amounts of time while they photocopy, rubber stamp and staple reams of paper, but they also send them on wild goose chases to obtain other documents from other public offices, despite knowing that the applicant will only be refused any immigration status at the end of the whole procedure anyway. This creates more public sector jobs for their friends and relatives. The Lord helps those who help themselves.

The Immigration Official glared over my shoulder at the Moroccan, who had tried to retake his rightful place at the head of the queue and was frogmarched away. He told me there were only three ways he could give me a 'Permesso di Soggiorno', or Permission of Stay Certificate. Either I had to be very rich, or I had to have a job in Sicily, or I had to marry a Sicilian.

"Exactly how rich?" I asked.

"Stinking," would be a loose translation of his answer.

"Go on, try me. Give me a number," I challenged him.

I had just sold my house in London so, as it turned out, I was that stinking rich. Both Hubby and the Immigration Official said declaring this level of wealth would be a terrible idea, because the government would spend the rest of my life trying to get every penny off me in the form of taxes I had never heard of. I went to that office about three times, to a couple of other ones a handful of times, and after a mere four months, I was legal.

What about the treatment of immigrants who come here not because they want to marry an Italian, but because they don't want to die?

Refugees in Lampedusa. Their detention centre looks a little cramped, doesn't it?

During the humanitarian crisis of the Libyan war, when Colonel Ghadaffi decided to kill all the sub-Saharan residents of Libya by using soldiers to physically propel them into the sea, Sicilian fishermen used to find groups of people swimming in the sea when they went out fishing at night.

What would you do if you were in a boat and saw the sea frothing with the waving arms of people struggling for their lives? Wouldn't you pull them aboard and take them ashore?

That would mean you just assisted illegal immigrants in entering the country. That's a crime.

A fishing boat in Lampedusa

And what if one of them was a pregnant woman who went into labour right in front of you on the beach? What you're supposed to do is call the police, who will arrest these people and take them to a detention centre where they will sleep in a dormitory with about 100 other people until they can be deported back to Africa as soon as possible. Except you know that the detention centre is already housing three times the number of people it was built for, so they will actually end up sleeping on the ground out of doors, and there are not enough blankets or clothes for them and there is also not enough drinking water.

Would you take that pregnant woman home to your wife instead, so she could give birth in safety? Then you'd be a criminal.

This is what happened to an Ethiopian refugee from Libya called Timnit. She was raped by prison guards when she was illegally detained in Libya, and she gave birth to her baby in a fisherman's house on the tiny Sicilian island of Lampedusa. This island, close to Sicily, is a little speck of paradise surrounded by the bluest azure seas and most dazzling of ultramarine skies in the world. When most people close their eyes and try to imagine paradise, the image in their mind is exactly what Lampedusa looks like.

Lampedusa has a population of 2,000 and their only source of income is tourism, which lasts two months in the summer. During these two months in 2011, 5,000 African refugees turned up from Libya. Every single one of them was fleeing for his or her life. Many of them died and their bodies still lie at the bottom of the sea.

The rest of Europe complains that Italy is a total pushover when it comes to illegal immigrants, or Clandestini, "The secret Ones" as they are more gently called in Italian. There are of course no border controls between countries of the European Union so, once one country has let immigrants or refugees in, they can go anywhere.

The Lampedusans pulled drowning Africans out of the sea whenever they could. They took blankets and every item of clothing they could spare, to give to the refugees. Almost no tourists went to Lampdeusa that year, which meant they lost their entire annual income.

The French decided to break EU law by closing their borders to trains from Italy. They sought and won EU approval for this. Then Berlusconi was attacked in Europe for his total lack of control or restriction over illegal immigration into the EU.

At this point Marine Le Pen, leader of the French National Front, took it upon herself to visit Lampedua personally and tell the Lampedusans they must stop letting Africans into Europe. The Lampedusans declared in advance on TV that they would be polite to her, as they are to all visitors to their island, but if she dared say anything racist or offensive they would reply to her in no uncertain terms.

Meanwhile the Lampedusans were running out of water. Refugees were sleeping on the beaches because there was physically no more space to cram any more of them into the detention centres. They were turning the beaches into mass open toilets because there was no more water to operate the sewage system, and no water for them to wash. Those who could get out of the detention centres did so, because the smell of excrement was intolerable. On 27 March 2011, a total of 1,227 new refugees arrived in the space of 24 hours.

This was the point when the Lampedusans complained. Why wouldn't the other European countries take more refugees? As many as possible had already been shipped to

Sicily and to the Italian mainland but the detention centres there were already filled three times over. If the other countries could spare planes and bombs to fight Ghadaffi's soldiers, why couldn't they save a few lives? Surely ALL countries had an equal moral responsibility to take some of them?

And what about America? That's what I say. Europe already has twelve times the population density of the United States. If you want to know what that means, transport the entire population of the USA, all the cities and all the people, into Oklahoma. Once all of them are living there, that's what it's like in Europe. How on earth, I mean, HOW ON EARTH, can Americans claim they don't have room for more refugees? How can they possibly complain about immigration? And please, don't tell me there's a money problem. America is richer than any European country. It's the richest country in the world.

The Lampedusans were told they would receive no help at all, and the refugees were not welcome in the rest of Europe or the rest of the world. Italy must send them back. This was the breaking point for the Lampedusans. When you have no clean water, and the fish you need to live on over the winter are dying because the sea has turned into a sewer, you have no choice, do you? So they went down to the harbour and, when the next boat full of African refugees tried to pull into port, they stood there shouting

"Please go away! We have no room for you here! You have to go somewhere else!"

And the boat sailed away.

A film called *Terraferma* was made in 2012 about Timnit and the other refugees who came to Sicily that year. Timnit herself acts in the film. The DVD with English subtitle is available from Amazon. I think that anyone who has ever complained about "too many immigrants" has a moral obligation to watch that film.

If you don't, frankly, you don't know what you're talking about.

Is Autumn EVER going to come?

"I can't wait for the leaves to turn red and golden and purple when autumn comes" my little boy announced a few days ago.

"Er, they won't go purple" I said.

"Yes they will," he insisted. "We're doing autumn at school and we wrote a poem about the leaves going purple."

Upon investigation of his school book, he admitted he had remembered the colours wrongly. The grapes are purple. The leaves go orange.

Of course the fundamental problem here was that he hadn't actually seen autumn leaves. As my best friend in Sicily - who comes from the far north of Italy - pointed out recently, in a state of great irritation, summer is brown in Sicily then as soon as autumn comes along, everything goes green.

"It's so, SO WRONG" we both agreed.

I got all excited a few weeks ago. It rained heavily and cooled off so much that I could actually wear my new cardigan for half the day. I dared to hope autumn might actually have arrived. Then the sun came out, the rain dried up, about twenty million new-born mosquitoes flew out of the puddles, and Sicily was back to normal; stinking hot, itchy, and a little bit smelly in places.

We are all getting so fed up that it has now become completely normal for strangers to say to other perfect strangers as they pass in the street "*Uffa*! I can't take it any more! WHEN are we going to get a bit of cool weather?!!" We are manifesting our impatience by creating bizarre outfits. Some people can be seen in T-shirts and woolly winter hats. I've seen a few young girls in vests, shorts and boots. "Phew! Just imagine the smell when she takes those off" was my husband's comment.

"Mummy, is it really true that the leaves go red and yellow in England when it's autumn?" my son asked me, not sounding completely convinced. I told him, when I was his age, we used to collect the colourful leaves and glue them on big pieces of paper to decorate the classroom with Autumnal collages.

"Wow!" he said. I had clearly impressed the socks off him.

Ah, what a gift from heaven!
But could you glue them on
sugar-paper to make a collage?

"Doing Autumn" in Sicily consists of learning all about how beautiful and wonderful grapes are, every squashy detail of how wine is made, and the name

124

of each part of a wine press. It spills into every subject. In Religion they learn how God gave us grapes as a special gift and we drink wine during mass as it is so precious. In Italian they copy poems about it. In Art Appreciation (yeah, Italian kids do art appreciation classes when they're six) they stick a still life by Caravaggio in their exercise book and write about the use of light and colour (purple!) in the original painting. In Science, they learn the name of every component of a grape vine. Did you know Italian has a special word for the tiny stalk that the grapes hang from, another word for the big stalk, and another one for the main stem of the plant? In Music Appreciation they are played "Autumn" from Vivaldi's Four Seasons while they draw any Autumnal scene they feel inspired to produce, and learn to identify the sounds of the musical instruments.

Could you name the Artist? Sicilians will think you're a Twit if you can't.

They go into the same level of detail on how olives are harvested and how oil is produced. I thought I knew this, roughly, but compared to all Sicilian seven-year olds I am an ignoramus! They label parts of oil presses and put the pictures in order. They learn words for olives that have been mushed up, and another word for the gubbins left over after you've pressed the extra virgin oil out but not done the second pressing to extract the oxidised, acidic junk you're going to sell to foreigners who don't know any better. There are about eight different verbs for different types of olive mashing, and my little boy knows them all. He even knows how to write them in joined up-writing. Some schools actually take the kids on outings at this time of year to see a local *frantoio* - that's the machine that presses the oil out.

A Frantoio..... could you label the parts? Really? In Italian?

This has made me realise how much of what we are taught at school creates the national culture. I think one way you could define a culture is "the stuff that just about everyone thinks is obvious". It's terribly difficult to work out just what this is, until you meet someone from another culture who doesn't know something that you have known for a very long time indeed.

When I was in primary school, I coloured in maps of Europe and learned each country and its capital. That's why we English always think Americans are incredibly stupid for not knowing the European countries. We don't actually stop to ask ourselves if we could reel off the capital of each of the states of America. (Actually, we could; it's just that we don't want to).

I memorised Bible stories with a relentless frenzy imposed by teacher after teacher. I am perpetually flabbergasted that Italian children do their first communion and all that, and come out of it not knowing one single bible story. I mean really, not one. They don't even know the proper details of the life of Jesus as told in the four gospels.

I spent lots of time learning about early British history. We did the Picts and Scots and Celts, we did the Romans, then we learned how the Angles, Saxons and Jutes invaded from Germany in the 5th century AD. That's why the British press mocked Mitt Romney, aka Mitt the Twit, after one of his aides made his "we have a shared Anglo-Saxon Heritage" comment in England. If he wanted to endear himself to us, reminding us that we once got invaded by a bunch of ruddy Germans was not a good plan. And anyway, what about all the other tribes?

(I would hate to mislead any American readers into thinking the UK is behind Obama and prefers him to Romney. In reality, Mr. Obama's carefully calculated Brit-antagonising antics have been so successful that we now hate him more than we ever hated Osama Bin Laden or Saddam Hussein. Surveys have shown that, among the younger generation, the majority believe the US is no longer worth pursuing as an ally; they feel we should focus efforts on wooing up-and-coming countries like India and China instead, which is more likely to succeed, and which will reap greater benefits in the long term.)

I could go on and on, but instead I need to make my son cut leaf shapes out of red, yellow and orange paper and turn them into a collage; I don't want him to grow up into the kind of twit who thinks Canadian Maple leaves turn violet in September.

Are our children beautiful enough?

A while ago, I asked my son what he wants to be when he grows up.
"I want to be fat," he answered without hesitation.
"Like the Daddy in the Simpsons," he explained.
"Like Obelix the Gaul," he emphasised.
"Like **him**", he exclaimed in delight when he saw Japanese hammer thrower Koji Murofushi in the Olympics. "Big, fat and very strong!" He delightedly launched his foam rubber hammer across the living room, imitating the throwing technique with uncanny accuracy.

I am sometimes glad I don't have a daughter. I have a friend whose 10 year old daughter is already worrying about being thin. She leaves half her dinner sometimes. She compares herself to the skinny girls at school and wishes she looked like them.

Half of me is not surprised about this. When you turn on Italian TV, this is what you typically see:

Not surprisingly, this is the doing of Berlusconi, who owns most Italian TV channels and, while president, indirectly controlled the rest.

The other half of me is shocked in disbelief that prepubescent children are already imposing this unhealthy nonsense on each other. At their age, dieting not only risks infertility and stunted growth but also irreparable organ damage. Children watch whatever adults watch nowadays. They copy everything with that total lack of criticism or judgement that is... well, typical of children.

The Italians used to be famous for their love of curvaceous women with big boobs, rounded hips and womanliness all over. Until recently, it was mandatory in all Italian movies for there to be one scene where the heroine, in her dangerously low-cut top, gets really pissed off about something and stomps away on her six inch heels, her boobs shown in close-up wobbling like a pair of jellies.

Sofia Loren   Gina Lollobrigida

Not any more. Nowadays, even in Italy, it's all about being thin. That means the women often get false boobs, which as we all know can't wobble even if their owner goes trampolining naked.

One of the things we women often tell each other, and which older women always tell younger girls whom they think are diet obsessed, is that men don't like those anorexic model types. They want "something to get hold of", we reassure each other. They like womanly women with boobs and curves, we claim hopefully.

But I am afraid that's not true any more. Men's opinions are influenced by the media just as much as women's. Seeing skinny actresses playing the role of the sex symbol gives men their idea of the kind of woman who will impress their friends, and thus, the kind of woman they want to date. Does anyone formulate their beauty ideal independently of the culture they live in? Almost nobody.

As I said, I am glad I don't have to worry about this. I'm glad to be the Mum of a little boy whose ambition is to be a fat and very strong hammer thrower. And, my God, he is so beautiful! Sometimes, I look at him when he's sleeping, and I get tears in my eyes to think how lucky I am.

We humans have always loved beauty. We have always wanted to be more beautiful. We have always favoured people we find beautiful and we always will. The only thing that changes over time is our definition of what is beautiful. Once it was this:

The Three Graces by Rubens. Note that the total removal of pubic hair has come back in, so maybe cellulite will soon have a fashion revival too

Nowadays, it's Angelina Jolie and other celebrities who look downright unhealthy.

It seems we can find just about any shape of human beautiful provided other humans tell us to do so. But can our definition of beauty *please* fall within the parameters of healthy?

Any responsible parent stops their children seeing sex or violence on TV. They are unsuitable for children. But what about those images that shape their idea of what is beautiful? Do we ever stop to consider if those are suitable?

As parents, we cannot just tell our teenage girls "Men like curves" or "Dieting at your age is unhealthy." If we ever need to say that to them, it's too late. Their beauty ideal has already been formed.

Good role models for YOUR daughter?

I don't have to worry about having an anorexic daughter in the future. But I don't want a git of a son either. I have decided to take control of what my boy sees on TV.

I do not allow terrestrial Italian TV to be switched on while my son is awake. I do not want my living room filled with images of unhealthily thin women dancing about in bikinis beside ugly, old, fully-clothed men who praise their beauty patronisingly, then ignore them while presenting a programme about what passes for politics in Italy.

My son may only be interested in cartoons so far, but what goes on in the background *does* influence children from the first day they see a television. I do not want my son to think that sexism is acceptable. I do not want him to think being thin equals being beautiful. I am determined that he will not grow up judging girls by how self-disciplined they are about dieting to below their natural weight.

I know a lot of other families in Italy who have made the same decision. I know some families who do not allow their teenage daughters to buy fashion magazines. And the number of parents making the same choices is growing. If all parents did that, the peer pressure at school would stop. If we all boycotted the fashion magazines and the unsuitable TV shows, they would eventually disappear.

We can blame the media but, in the end, we as parents CAN have control over what influences our children. We just have to take it.

Questionnaire: How Sicilian are you?

I have been delighted over the year to learn how many Sicilians are enjoying my blog. It seems those who live here, and the expats who have fled to the USA and other places, are equally happy to be mocked mercilessly.

Some of them have indicated that they now straddle two cultures and feel nostalgic about the Sicilian characteristics they remember in more elderly relatives. Meanwhile, most foreign expats here in Sicily notice sooner or later that, unlike myself, they are getting somewhat Sicilianised. And what about the genuine mixtures like my son? Are they still English? Or are they more Sicilian?

Personally, I can assure you I am still more English than an egg cosy. But for everyone else, the whole situation can become confusing. I think this personality questionnaire may help to clarify for each and every one of you, just how Sicilian are you?

A Sicilian

Some Egg Cosies

QUESTIONS

1. *It is a sunny day and 24 degrees outside. Do you....?*
A) Immediately put on your shorts, call all your friends round to your house for a barbecue and serve them charred embers which can be cracked open to reveal that they actually have a core of raw chicken marinated in lighter fuel
B) Go for a walk in the park

C) Dress yourself and your child in seven anoraks, rush to the car and drive to the pharmacy for cough medicine, complaining bitterly to anyone you meet that this atrocious weather has given your entire family the flu, fevers and bronchitis and will be the end of you all before the winter is out

2. *It is 41 degrees outside and the sun is melting the tarmac. Do you....?*
A) Do nothing – you are delirious with heat stroke
B) Go to the beach and cool off in the sea
C) Get seven chickens, two lambs and five goats out of your freezer, buy a calf from the butcher and a truck of vegetables and invite all your friends and family over for a barbecue, so you can have a good chat standing round the fire all afternoon

3. *Your best friend is getting married. To celebrate the joyous occasion, would you dress in...?*
A) A frock covered in pastel coloured flowers and a large hat with a fake rose on the side
B) A chic new outfit you have splashed out on for the occasion
C) A full-length black evening gown dripping with black sequins, a black shawl, a black lace head covering, black stockings, black shoes and a pair of dark, black, black, black, black, black sunglasses from Gucci's new Summer collection

4. *Your car is...?*
A) A Ford that you'll be paying instalments on for the next seven years
B) A Japanese car that has low petrol consumption
C) A Fiat Punto with over eighty dents in the body work, a string of rosary beads dangling off the rear view mirror and a medallion of Padre Pio glued on the windscreen where the tax disc should be

5. *You are travelling through the countryside and see a mangy, moth-eaten looking horse in a muddy field. Do you...?*
A) Cry, and then sign over your life savings, your house and your children's college fund to "Save Mildewed Horses from the Knackers" registered charity No.17974
B) Nothing – it seems to be in no pain
C) Attach a two-foot-long plume of multi-coloured ribbons to its head, yoke it up to a luminous yellow cart and goad it with a sharp stick until it is cantering at 95 miles an hour down the centre of a dual carriageway

6. *Your job is...?*
A) Something you have just lost
B) Boring but a way of paying the bills, and you hope it will last through the recession
C) Part-time work as a cleaner that you have been doing for 17 years and they still haven't given you a contract but you feel lucky to have it as a source of income... even though you actually have a degree in Astro-physics

7. *You a walk into your kitchen and notice a bit of dirt on the floor. Do you...?*
A) Step over it on your way to the kettle
B) Wipe it up with a cloth and a squirt of Ajax
C) Cancel all social engagements for the next three days, dress up in a hideous flowery pinny with frills round the armpits and get out 27 bottles of ammonia, bleach and other cleaning products powerful enough to make you hallucinate and scrub down the ceiling, walls and floor with a set of wire scrubbing brushes in 12 different sizes

8. *You are sitting in the living room when you hear your child sneeze. Do you...?*
A) Say "Bless you"
B) Offer him a tissue
C) Scream and faint, dress him in 27 anoraks and a blanket, start hyperventilating and drive up the hard shoulder of the motorway all the way to the nearest casualty department, where you barge past the triage nurse and insist he is put on a drip and an oxygen mask and treated with a cocktail of antibiotics until you get kicked out 2 hours later. Then, text 750 of your closest relatives and friends to invite them to a special thanksgiving mass to thank Santa Rosalia of Monte Pellegrino for rescuing him from the jaws of death.

9. *Your country has just won the World Cup. Would you...?*
A) Wonder how on earth you travelled in time right back to 1966
B) Celebrate with friends over a few beers
C) Spontaneously form a slow-moving procession through town, beeping the horn of your Fiat Punto or your farty little Vespa non-stop and banging saucepans together. Then go to some all-night café with your mates and have a fried spleen sandwich and a drink of coffee out of a ceramic thimble.

10. *You have just met a girl you fancy. Do you...?*
A) Act like a total nerd and ignore her in front of your friends
B) Bring her cups of tea and try to make her laugh lots
C) Shower her with shiny gifts, cook her a twenty course dinner, tell her that her eyes look like two stars fallen from heaven and then give her a glass of champagne to get her tipsy before you move in for a snog?

11. *Your house is...?*
A) A semi that is now worth less than half what you paid for it
B) A rented flat
C) A concrete cube that looks like a public toilet with lumps of masonry falling off the outside, but with an interior like Buckingham Palace (only much cleaner).

12. *You decide to have a day at the beach. Do you...?*
A) Roll your trousers up to mid-calf length or tuck you skirt into your knickers at the side, balance a knotted hanky on your head and paddle in the freezing water for five minutes, then have fish and chips in a deck chair with a mug of tea from your thermos flask

B) Swim a bit, sunbathe a bit and hope you don't get burned

C) Pack a picnic of 25 sandwiches a yard long, eight cream cakes and several roasted chickens, seafood salad, biscuits and anything else in your kitchen and sit in the sun eating the lot, then charge down the beach and throw yourself at the water, creating a tsunami that obliterates Sardinia

13. *You are getting ready for a night out. Do you...?*

A) Scratch'n'sniff your armpits to see how smelly they are before rummaging through your combat trouser pockets for your Oyster card

B) Have a shower and put on something smart

C) Wash for four hours, put a whole tub of gel on your hair, pour three full bottles of aftershave over yourself then dress from head to toe in colour-coordinated clothes

14. *Your little sister is..?*

A) A bit of a pain sometimes

B) A good laugh

B) Who wants to know? What's his name and where does he live? Tell me where I can find him.

RESULTS

Mostly A

We're sorry, but there is not a Sicilian cell in your body. You are so English that, if you went to Sicily, they would call you "Milord", tell you your compatriots are all "cold and closed" and then offer you a cup of tea in an egg cup, showing you a packet of tea the size of a matchbox that someone brought back from a holiday to London in 1982 which now tastes of nothing more than mild gerbil poo.

Mostly B

You are the perfect hybrid. You and your relatives are frequently to be found on the Ryanair flight between Palermo and Stansted, talking fluent cockney on the way out and fluent Sicilian on the way back. Your name is something like Totò Thompson or Gary Gambino and you are equally happy eating fish and chips or spleen sandwiches, it's all the same to you as long as it's fatty.

Mostly C

Congratulations! You are a thoroughbred Sicilian. It is not possible to be more Sicilian than you. In fact, you are so Sicilian that we cannot believe you actually speak enough English to have done this test yourself. You must have cheated…. which only goes to prove, even more, how very Sicilian you are.

DID YOU ENJOY THIS BOOK?

If you enjoyed this book, please go to Amazon and write a glowing review or, better still, persuade some of your friends to buy more copies of it.
The author is skint and would be so grateful.

You could also try my other books.....

Available in paperback and Kindle on Amazon websites worldwide

The Dangerously Truthful Diary of a Sicilian Housewife

An English woman takes on parenthood, the Mafia and a Sicilian mother-in-law, all at once

AMAZON BESTSELLER

When career-girl Veronica flies to Sicily for a friend's wedding, she accidentally falls in love with one of the groom's three-hundred cousins. A year later she has given up her job, house and friends, and is planning her own wedding with her Latin Lover in the shimmering heat of Sicily.

She suspects her seaside dream-villa is being built by the Mafia when the stubbly foreman visits, brandishing a large hammer and demanding more money. In shock, she learns her Sicilian spleen-sandwich and prickly-pear cravings are because she is pregnant. Still reeling, Veronica is challenged to a duel fought with wooden spoons over who is the better woman, when her rosary-flailing mother-in-law starts checking her son's vests are ironed and inspecting the toilet bowl for subtle skidmarks.

Can resourceful Veronica solve her problems by pitching one adversary against the other?

Join her on an unpredictable journey of hilarity, reckless driving and dangerously large portions of spaghetti in this almost true travel-novel, for people who need more belly-laughs.

"The diary is filled with biting wit, an astute knack for observation and a powerful sense of determination which makes it a joy to read. Di Grigoli's strong personality comes out as she deftly sketches out the intricacies of life on the complex island of Sicily at the heart of the Mediterranean."
TIMES OF SICILY

"A laugh out loud book about my favourite Mediterranean island. Warmly recommended to all travellers to that Sicily. Just read this for the second time and enjoyed it even more for the author's wit, her love of the people of the village and the island, and for her acute understanding of the reasons they are what they are. What makes a Sicilian? Ask Veronica, she'll tell you."
AMAZON REVIEWER

I bought a Kindle copy of this wonderful book... I sat down on the floor (next to the charger) and started reading... and reading... and laughing and laughing. ...this is a gem of a book that reminds me, in all the very best ways, of one of my favourite traveling authors Gerald Durrell. Veronica Di Grigoli brings Sicily to hilarious and colourfully informative life – I'm only sorry that I'm not traveling there tomorrow! It's very hard to write humor well, but she does it extraordinarily and effortlessly well."
YANGSZE CHOO, AUTHOR

Evil Eye

When naïve English teacher Celeste blunders into a dangerous web of mystery in hypnotic Istanbul, the only way to save herself is by saving someone else first

Freshly graduated and orphaned at the same time, day-dreamy Celeste is hypnotised by the ethereal mosques and dazzling bazaars of Istanbul as an escape from all that hurts her. Yet running away from her problems only leads her into new ones.

Her students at the swanky language school seem more interested in their manicures than her English lessons. The morose caretaker of the orphanage where she volunteers stares at her boys like a vulture sizing up its next meal. Worst of all, her landlady lets slip sinister comments that don't make sense, leaves spine-chilling mystic charms around the house, and puts magic spells in places she should not be going.

When Celeste's favourite orphan vanishes, she embarks on a frantic search through crowded bazaars and dangerous alleys, desperate to find one small boy lost in a city of ten million. But can innocent Celeste save the child, and herself, before someone destroys them?

"This is the first book I read by veronica Di Grigoli and I loved the atmosphere of Istanbul that it provoked. Even though it's a story of danger and tension, it made me really want to visit the city – though I almost feel as if I have after reading this. I liked the way the book featured various different female characters – the mothers, daughters, women without children – the subtle way their attitudes and characters are shown is really thought-provoking far beyond the actual story in the book. It's the kind of book that stays on your mind for a long time after you've read it."
AMAZON REVIEWER

Friends with Secrets

What do an English teacher and an investment banker have in common? If they want to live, everything.

New York, 1993: Mistry thinks she has a safe job in a bank, but when she realises a client is using her to launder money, someone tries to kill her. How can she outwit a criminal who has already outwitted the police?

London, England: College teacher Crystal befriends a teenage language student from war-torn Georgia as he confides in her how his brother was kidnapped and held to ransom. A Colombian student, realising she has spotted him receiving a huge sum of cash, threatens to kill her if she tells the police. When another student vanishes, Crystal realises she has stumbled into a deadly conflict between a Colombian drug cartel and the Soviet Mafia. She already knows too much. Who can help her now?

As the net tightens around Crystal, and Mistry's assassin tries to kill her again, they cross paths and realise their only hope is to unite forces. Two scared young women discover just how resourceful danger can make them. But are they in time to save each other's lives?

"This is a tense thriller where the two protagonists are both women and the plot whizzes along at a fast pace, yet the author still builds up the characters and relationships between them so it is not just a plot-driven story, but has quite a lot of subtlety to it."
AMAZON REVIEWER

Printed in Great Britain
by Amazon